STATE CHAMP

STATE CHAMP

A NOVEL

HILARY PLUM

BLOOMSBURY PUBLISHING

NEW YORK · LONDON · OXFORD · NEW DELHI · SYDNEY

BLOOMSBURY PUBLISHING
Bloomsbury Publishing Inc.
1359 Broadway, New York, NY 10018, USA
50 Bedford Square, London, WC1B 3DP, UK
Bloomsbury Publishing Ireland Limited,
29 Earlsfort Terrace, Dublin 2, D02 AY28, Ireland

BLOOMSBURY, BLOOMSBURY PUBLISHING, and the Diana logo are
trademarks of Bloomsbury Publishing Plc

First published in the United States 2025

ISBN: HB: 978-1-63973-543-3; EBOOK: 978-1-63973-544-0

LIBRARY OF CONGRESS CATALOGING-IN-PUBLICATION DATA IS AVAILABLE

2 4 6 8 10 9 7 5 3 1

Typeset by Westchester Publishing Services
Printed in the United States by Lakeside Book Company, Harrisonburg, VA

Bloomsbury books may be purchased for business or promotional use.
For information on bulk purchases please contact Macmillan Corporate
and Premium Sales Department at specialmarkets@macmillan.com.
For product safety related questions contact productsafety@bloomsbury.com.

for Caryl & Caren & Alyssa & Jess

& in remembrance

for Marie

We have different relationships to windows.

MELISSA DICKEY

Day 2

I'm going to use all the printer paper.

No, Donna, I'm not using both sides.

No, I'm not starting with day 1.

Anyone who counts day 1 of a hunger strike is not going to make it. You just ate.

I'm at work. I'm living here. I thought it through. It's October, even if someone shuts off the heat it won't get cold for a while. Plenty of time. No one's allowed to live here, zoning, but if they haul me out they'll just bring me to jail, which works. No one's allowed to do abortions here anymore, but me I'm just sitting in a room. Water and lights are paid through December, I think. Or at least through the end of the month. There's a sort of shower in the back, a nozzle in the wall. I brought a lot of bottled water. No food. Keep it simple. I slept on an examination table last night, in your old sleeping bag. Inside near the top smelled like coconut. Sunscreen, I guess. Further down smelled like rainwater, like that Velcro sound when you pin back the tent flap and look for stars. John, you're always prepared. You always own the right stuff already. I don't know how that works, it's like you went shopping at birth. I stole this sleeping bag from you last time I saw you. It's hard to steal something shaped like a sleeping bag but that's my skill set. I didn't have a purpose in mind, back then, I just wanted to try out your lifestyle. And now here I am, prepared. For example I brought—I rode the bus here so it was not easy—a bunch of buckets, now filled with water and lined up in the hallway. The hallway that was too narrow to fit a gurney with doctors suited up on both sides, like on TV, running while they ask the patient overly emotional questions, except you could just push it from behind, it's a very short hallway, you could honestly just carry someone to the end of it honeymoon-style, I know because one night after the holiday thing Monica tried it with me, Monica scooped me up and carried me, we were both drunk but it went fine, you can save more lives drunk than you ever dreamed. Hallway width was one of the first restrictions. A million tiny laws and big court cases later and we had to open up a sort of loading dock area in the back, like truckfuls of knocked-up humans would be rolled down in here, babies sucked out of them. Exit through the front. The buckets are in case the water gets cut. I want to be able to flush the toilet. I honestly don't know what the situation of shitting will be. I'm guessing major, then nothing. I did shit yesterday. Day 1. I thought there was something already wrong with me then remembered, beets. I had a big old beet salad, last day of gluttony. I have not shit today. I feel hungry, which I'm hoping will stop soon, like how you get warm as you freeze. They say. My breath is very bad and I find that interesting. Whenever I've dieted hard-core the breath rots right away, like it knows what you're thinking. Blasting out the passage. Can teeth melt? My tongue's a little stinker. Like nothing could ever taste good. I bet this paper smells like my breath.

Whoever is reading this, give it to John. It's for John, I should have said.

John, I wrote and called you yesterday. You're an OK reporter. You're pretty good, I think. You wrote me back *wtf u for real* which is not what a good reporter would write but on the other hand made us both feel dramatic. My aunt, who would like to remind you she is a city councilwoman, who I emailed to be official, has been calling all day. I'm not answering. I'm just sending her selfies. In the latest, I'm drinking water, slice of lemon, out of a urine sample cup. I brought the lemons, that's not food. She can tell from the photo I am where I say I am. Now I just have to chill. Yesterday I sat on the floor and stretched for so long I think my hamstrings liquified. The rug smells like comfy shoes worn by scared women.

This strike is for Dr. M, who was sentenced last week.

Should have said that on page 1.

She can't hunger strike because of her diabetes. She actually said exactly this once, *too bad for me, I could never go on a hunger strike because of my diabetes.* 12 years minimum, 12 years before parole, that's what she's got going now. 10 would be plenty but they went in for the extra 2. I don't know what she'll do in there. As far as I can tell she's never even thought about something that wasn't work. Maybe she'll be roomed with another abortion doc and they can set a professional tone. Sew tags into mall-brand bras, but like at a high level?

That I'm here at work and she isn't is kind of ironic, or is it a paradox, since Dr. M does not in general have a lot of confidence in me, which I know because she has on more than one occasion made lots of eye contact with me while saying *Angela, I find I do not have a lot of confidence in you.* But I think this is the one task she might bet on me for, since she always, and I liked it, did remember that I was "an athlete." Her son was a few years ahead of me in high school and played tennis famously. So she'd follow the high school sports coverage. Even though he was long gone, off at college, I'm sure already doing something useful like inventing a vaccine to prevent fellow geniuses from getting tattoos they'd regret later when their dad bods set in. I don't think Dr. M has ever had a habit she didn't keep up with. I bet she still plays with dolls just to keep her hand in the game. Dr. M can tell winners from losers. So she'd remember, if I was reaching up for a ream of printer paper on the shelf and gave a little hop, she would say, *there you go, Angela, very athletic. I haven't forgotten you were a state champion.*

It's really paying off, I'd say, or something.

Well, you didn't do it for the reward, she said once, and she was right actually. I can right now taste the waste of puking hard onto green grass, in the middle of a random field, walking it off after getting out of the finish-line chute, kind of careening forward along the ropes and water-cup people until you're finally out in the open and you can finally puke. My point is, I think this is a paradox not an irony because it comes from something we both understand, me and Dr. M. I think irony is like, not knowing + someone else watching = knowing. But what about knowing + knowing = the opposite of what you thought you knew. John, you're the writer. John, help me out.

Day 3

Krys was right. There are roaches. A guy came last spring to genocide them, but no. Who knows what he killed, the roaches are fine. Every other day, right as I got in, Krys would be talking about how she was the first one here, and when she flicked the light on in the break room she'd hear roach feet cackling toward the walls. I wasn't here in time to squeal with her, was her point. Even if I did get here first, I told her, I wouldn't go to the break room because I don't pack a lunch. Krys was always putting her cute purple lunch sack in the fridge, sandwich sliced into quarters and a little baby Coke. She uses those baggies that fold over at the top, don't zip shut, real act of faith in plastic. The break room is kind of your thing, I pointed out, so the roaches are kind of your thing. People always want to make jobs about something else that's not even the job. *How are you so skinny?* Krys or Monica or whoever would say. *You eat so unhealthy. You always eat crap.* People shouldn't ask questions they don't want answered.

I hear the roaches at night. I hear their whole civilization. If they had a roach abortion clinic with roach protestors, I'd know all about it. I brought roach spray. I thought of that, so thanks, Krys. Now that I'm not eating it's good to still be killing at least one animal.

This morning I found a roach floating in the bucket closest to the break room. I was going to get a pair of latex gloves, fish it out, chuck it. There's the parking lot dumpster. But I keep hearing about microplastics in the ocean. There's more tiny plastic pieces now than plankton? You go to get a big mouthful of little food critters with your cool whale mouth and it's plastic plastic plastic. On the news they just rescued a turtle from some beach and it shit plastic for days. So I used my bare hands, I fished the roach out by its leg, but that didn't work, so I touched its whole wet bug self. Hunger-strike-wise, anything that grosses you out is just fuel to the fire. Little roach baby, I said, though it was probably a roach mama, did you ever think that when they closed down the abortion clinic, you'd die too? No lunches, no Wednesday donuthole boxes? And here I am with no food. So this is how it ends. I flicked the corpse into the trash and drops of water flicked back off its dead wings at my face. Christ. Were they—they weren't—eating, like, tissue? They weren't. Everything's sealed off, disposed of right. We used to have to prove this, and then things got even weirder, and we had to ask the people lying there on the table, legs in stirrups, *hey, did you want the fetal tissue buried or cremated?* I never asked that myself, I just heard about it. I'm sure they asked ahead of time, not right in the middle. Monica said most people started panicking, they wanted you to decide, or say what's normal. But you had to tell them, no, the person getting the procedure is required to determine the method of disposal.

Someone thought of this law.

But roaches get us all eventually, right? Eventually everyone is something bugs eat.

I don't think anyone else is still protesting for Dr. M. People will keep protesting the heartbeat law, or the next law up, which will ban every abortion in this state forever. After the heartbeat law that one's sort of unnecessary but they'll go for it. If other states are going all 1800s, we've got to keep up. But everyone's already forgetting about Dr. M. All the talk of bans and referendums and how the referendums will get blocked, it all drowns her out. She's just a name you'd list somewhere, another shitty or great thing that happened. Her sentence came down last week, but it was just a sad blip in the news. That's why I'm here, why I'm starting something. Because it's like, where's Dr. M's baby boy? Where's everyone who cared so much for a minute?

During her trial twin crowds corralled outside the courthouse. Once or twice I joined in. I'm not much of a sign waver. I didn't know what to bring. I knew I'd duck out early and in the meantime I just kind of stood there till Donna gave me pamphlets to hand out.

If we're being honest, only Donna was talking to me then. Or now. The others were pissed because they thought I'd made things worse. They thought I'd snitched. They were wrong but it's not the kind of thing I could just explain. They don't think I can handle myself. But the thing with the politician's aide was just fucking, which is exactly the sort of thing I can handle.

Didn't help that I hated the pamphlets, which were just like government office numbers to call, places to donate to. This is great for other people, was my point, but for Dr. M, it was like everyone had already given up on her, like only the cause mattered and not the individual people, when individual people were the cause anyway, like *everyone who walks through our doors*, the phrase Donna used to say . . .

At the trial, in the crowd opposite us, outside the courthouse, lined up on the sidewalk and basically high-fiving each other, were some of the old shouters. Back from the dead. It was weird to recognize them. All those guys who used to show up with baseball caps that said *Repent Whore* (who needs punctuation), homemade signs against *Muslims and Homos* ("Are you lost? This is just an abortion clinic," I told a guy once, then had to like wash his reply out of my ears), blown-up cut-up fetus signs, signs tallying some number of babies dead since '73. Last time that sign got waved at me I said, "God, I've had my period way more than that and I'm only 27." (28.) I regret saying that since I think most people think I'm younger than I am. And to be honest I'm not much of a menstruater.

Janine, though, Janine is the queen of flow, everyone syncs their cycles up to hers. Janine was outside the courthouse every day. She kept her distance from the *Repent Whore* crowd (they do not smell great) and sometimes the guys seemed like they were shouting not just at Dr. M and us but at her, with a kind of pissed-off flirtation she seemed into. Whatever battle had taken place between these factions, for the right to scream at human beings all day in our parking lot, she'd won. For years those dudes assigned themselves to us, showing up whenever they felt like it, messaging consistent, membership inconsistent, led by an old priest who, someone said, was in the midst of a big heap of accusations for child sexual abuse. Allegedly. Do you have to say allegedly in your personal hunger journal? Anyway like three years ago Janine and her girls showed up, and not long after we never saw the old shouters and that bummer of a priest again. Turf turnover. Janine runs a tight ship. I swear I did not hear the word *whoremonger* from the day she took over the parking lot until the trial's cool generational mix. *Repent Whores* were Facebook, Janine was Instagram. On fall days she wore sweater blazers and they were shapely. Her girls handed out well-formatted pamphlets and cute rubber baby dolls, talked less about *babykillers* and more about *resources. We're here to empower women*, they'd say. *Society is pressuring you*, they'd say, *but you're free to listen to your heart*, and they'd press this cute swaddled rubber baby, pink ribbon round its torso, into your hand, really wedge it in there. No more fake-blood-smeared dolls hurled at someone's face. *We're here to save lives and love women.* You could see Janine monitoring each member of her little team, approving their message, syllable by syllable. The minute Dr. M was arrested, funnily about nine months ago now, Janine must have known she'd won. She preened outside the courthouse, there to see and be seen, hair dyed dark red, darker than blood and glinting.

When I scrolled through photos from the news, two crowds doing their thing in front of the courthouse, I saw someone I hadn't seen there in person. Rose, standing to the side of the crowd, looking like I must have looked, like she didn't want to get closer, didn't know what to do. Just standing there wearing a windbreaker over jean shorts so short they were more of a rumor, her legs kind of knock-kneed, thigh faintly yellow.

In the waiting room she'd tipped her head back to rest on the wall, exposing her neck, which looked long and throbbing, like you could see her pulse going hard in the side of it, like a thumb had pressed into the freaked-out heart of this weak clay. At the desk she'd started to tell me everything, lots of people do that, I have to break in to tell them I'm not a nurse or anything, they can wait to talk to the nurse when they go back. Sometimes it's true I could interrupt faster. Sometimes Monica would step in and keep her eye on me, saying, "Oh she doesn't have medical training, but we'll help you with all of that in the back." A few months before Dr. M's arrest Rose had come up to the desk gripping her clipboard, left wrist choked with little beaded bright bracelets like kids make, she's a real sport for wearing those around. She'd been in for a procedure and now she was back for birth control. She had the prescription but she didn't like it. "Is there a stronger pill? I need a stronger pill," she was saying.

"I hear you," I said. "The nurse—"

"I don't get my period with this one," she was saying, "and I need to get my period, I'm spending like so much money on tests—"

"It's all about the estrogen," I said. "They'll totally—"

"I have to get my period."

I think it all got sorted out, except now we're closed and she'll have to get her pill somewhere else, we can't help anyone. I keep thinking the phone will ring and I'll be able to help someone, by chance, by still being here, just picking up the phone. Everyone in the world doesn't know everything that happened, someone could just call, thinking we're still here, ready to help, whatever they need. But what could I do anyway, what would I say? Before the heartbeat law passed, people were calling and calling. Like from other states where the laws had moved faster. You'd ask for an address and it was like, what? If I got up to take a piss I'd miss like ten calls. Sometimes when you picked up the phone to dial, there'd just be someone there already, *hello?* I started making outgoing calls on my cell while the actual phone rang in my face.

And then after the heartbeat law, mostly if I answered I was just like, no. You can come in and see. But if you already know and you're already too far along . . . No no no no no no no. Then Dr. M was like, *take down their names anyway. Try to get them in anyway. If there's even a chance*, she'd say, *they could have the dates wrong, some crisis pregnancy center could have told them wrong . . .*

"Get their info, I'll call them back," she said. That should have tipped me off?

"Dr. M," I said, "have you tried using the phone? Pick that shit up and see what happens."

"Just get their information, Angela. As many as you can."

And now there was an outgoing message on the system. I know because I recorded it. Donna kept trying to leave the message on the last day. It felt like there were a million last days, we stayed open after the law flipped, we stayed open after the heartbeat law passed, we kept doing all the things that weren't the main thing, seeing patients, pills, exams, referrals, more referrals, and every day felt like both the absolute last day and the day after the last day, like a sort of hell where you tried to catch up on everything everyone ever alive hadn't gotten done, but anyway then Dr. M got arrested, the money got frozen or tied up or whatever and there were more search warrants and we were fucked. It was done. So on the last last day Donna kept starting to leave a message then getting too choked up, not a problem I expected Donna to have. "I can't do it," she said. "Krystal, can you do it?" Krys had come in to take down all her identical beach sunset photos and her actually framed and signed *Hamilton* poster and she was asking Donna about medical supplies, what the cops took, what would be donated. She had a box in her hands when Donna called out to her. "I'm busy," she said to Donna, "have Ange do it." She could see I was sitting at the big desktop, where I happened to be deleting some browser history. Way too late. "All we're doing is telling them they're screwed, they have to try to get out of state in time? Have Ange do it, Ange always sounds like a stone-cold bitch."

So yeah, it's my voice, I'm the one who breaks the news. We're gone, we're shut down, welcome to no one helping you ever, nope, no voicemail. But I'm the one here now, still here. Huh. But to Rose that doesn't matter. The pills are all gone and for all the times Dr. M said it was *such a simple procedure* she never taught us. That was a rule she didn't break.

Day 4

Hungry.

No surprise but real sick.

Bored.

Horny?

Don't you get bored? they'd ask me about like the 5K, 10K, all the distance stuff, 25 laps around the track. *I would be so bored.* No. I don't *get* bored, I was already bored. Pain distracts you from being bored and god do you need that. I think the great runners are all like this, if they talk about focus or a runner's high they're lying. Compared to being bored you were less scared of pain. To do something scary you just need to be more scared of something else.

We're all bored, but I'm fast. Was fast? I've been trying to do the old push-up/sit-up thing but this morning I just lay for a while face down on the rug. Mostly I've been scrolling Instagram and farting. I have to keep moving rooms. I'd post if I could post a fart.

Right now I'm wanting a hot bowl of those baked beans from a can, lick your finger as you crank the lid off, slices of hot dog cooked up in butter that you tumble on into the bowl of beans, *pennies*, my mom called them, cooked so the hot dog skin peels away from the meat of the bite. Fuck.

As you can see, John, I got bored with printer paper and I'm using the exam table paper. Scrolling it out on the grimy tile floor. Exam room 1, but I'm going to try them all. Writing with one of our shitty pencils. At around 4 or 5, happy hour, Dr. M might stab a pencil through the thick of her bun, angled like 2 to 8 o'clock in bun-time. Her hair must go down past her waist. If middle age dries it out, you can't tell. She must oil it, there's a scent if she leans over the desk and her braid swings at you. She dyes the shit out of it. Unflinchingly black. When does she find the time? Some salon must open at like 3 a.m. Dr. M, we give those pencils to patients, I'd say, it's not sanitary. This one's for me, she'd say, but she'd leave it wherever. She'd spin a pencil in her fingers for an hour at staff meetings, bored at a meeting she'd called. I don't think she ever wrote with one because they suck to write with.

During the trial her roots came in, hard.

Put your hand here, on the belly. I love when the belly retreats from the hips. The world's gone from you, the world's left outside you. It's like a low tide. The skin is sinking, soft and low. You can feel the fine ropey fibers, intricate. Like whatever lies below the sea's surface, greening the light.

Glow, everyone says that about pregnant women. Lots of people look fucking sick. The baby isn't some sacred candle lit from the perfect flame of the body. *Radiant.* The baby is competition, a second call you get while you're putting out a housefire. To make its bones the baby just sucks out your bones. I'm not against it. But don't lie about it.

Whenever people say a woman looks good, guaranteed she was puking or shitting her guts out like moments before. Exception for when there's not enough left in there. Been there, getting there. Beauty means you're a little too empty and you want to be a little too full, you're ready for anyone to pack their bullshit back in you. You look so, like, receptive. Walking the runway like sticking your little hand through the cage.

John, I haven't texted you since day 1. I'm waiting. It's pathetic. I'm not going to write you like, *I know you have a lot going on.* Like, *I'm actually dying just thought you'd wanna know thx.* You didn't write about Dr. M's trial so I guess that's not your beat or whatever. Whoever wrote about her in your cheap paper kept saying *abortion doctor.* You could just say she's a doctor. She wasn't just hosing and scraping uteruses out all day.

To explain how it worked once she made a gesture with her hand in the air. Moved her hand in the air between us like the air was a womb. I can't tell if my memory's fucked but I think, right then, I was turned on. For a sec. Or I'm turned on now and that's like obscuring the record. If she moves her hand in the air, I remember how my hips were propped on your lap in the back of your car. Your whole hand was in me. Usually I don't know how many fingers—you laughed once when I asked, *how many fingers*, but how would I know?—but I could feel it this time, your whole hand cupped downward and fingers moving together, a deep wave that went to the heart of each nerve. Like say you're making a dandelion crown as a kid and you get bored, you split the stem of one dandelion and keep slicing it long all the way up to the blossom, white milk sticky under your nail. I came right into your fist. You showed me your palm when you pulled it out, flicked it half-clean out the car door, onto the asphalt, I guess. You got out to smoke. I lay there for a sec then I joined you. You always gave me my very own cigarette like we hadn't just fucked. It was bright out. Sometimes you seemed nervous about being seen and I couldn't tell if that was stage fright or if you had a girlfriend and didn't want to get caught. I don't usually ask questions. I'm never sure what I'm supposed to learn.

Angela, if you don't know how to do something, why don't you just ask?

Angela, people would like you better if you asked them questions about themselves. You have to show interest.

"Dr. M's finishing school for lifetime receptionists," I said. She looked at me calmly, but like it cost her.

"You know, Angela," she said, "I have worked as a receptionist. For several years, in Pakistan, in a doctor's office, before I became a doctor myself. I had to use a typewriter."

I tipped my head to the side. I did not ask a question.

"I bet you were good at it," I said. "But I bet the other girls didn't like you."

She took a long pause, but that doesn't work on me. I love time.

"You make a good point, Angela," she said. "No, I would say they did not."

Ever think of Rose who showed up one year in early spring, I remember snowdrops were blooming along the curb of the parking lot island, and I was feeling good until I walked in late, got yelled at, *LATE!* and halfway through the day I had to count Rose's cash out to give back to her, I guess I shouldn't have taken it in the first place, too late for Rose, I should have known, but how would I know? At the end of her appointment, which was short, I gave back the exact same damp bills she'd brought in. Threshold of viability, crossed. "Sorry I had to change the appointment," she'd said, when I'd checked her in and she'd handed a wad of bills to me, "I hadn't finished raising the money yet." One of those funds had helped her but it's not enough, and now *your money's no good here*, I didn't say. The price had gone up since we'd first quoted it, weeks and weeks back, she'd crossed into the second trimester. And now, too late, the third. I didn't ask if she'd have to give the money all back to someone somewhere, probably, or could she keep it to use for the kid or at least the time off to deliver. She didn't look pissed. I wouldn't say pissed. She'd zipped her purple fleece up snug against her chin, she nestled her chin in as she watched me fish out the cash. She looked like she'd just learned she'd been totally right about something important, too late, now that it no longer mattered. "I gotta get home," she said when I finished counting. I don't think I said anything since none of my preprogrammed speeches—*call us with questions, let's schedule your next appointment*—made sense. But I slipped her an extra $20 out of the drawer.

Day 5

I'll call the police, my aunt texted me.

No you won't, I texted back. *Pls call a newspaper.*

I know she remembers my record because she brings it up every chance she gets. Like Donna saying extra loud when I'm late *I know you don't drive but the bus runs every half hour.* Or: *You know we were supposed to hire someone with a degree and we took a chance on you.* Or just: *You know you're lucky to have this job.* You're lucky you can mention my background to sound so enlightened, I wanted to say.

The bus makes me think of those big-ass coffee drinks, embarrassing, the ones that are all sugar and ice and some fake flavor that tastes burned and druggy, and you get a big straw so at the end you can suck the ice crystals up, drag the last sugar up with them, shake the cup and suck suck suck. The coffee place was right by my second-favorite bus stop but I only splurged sometimes, every now and then, medium no whip, way too much money, god I would love that shit right now, OK moving on.

Anyway I sent three photos to my aunt, mug-shot-style: me facing left, center, right. No smiling. Bags under the eyes were almost actually blue.

I need to talk to the papers.

I've been told I need to work on my "communication skills." Also my "people skills." Which is it, people?

If the clinic was too busy or not busy at all I sometimes walked patients back. I can tell when someone's about to lose it and not in a welling-up blink-it-out kind of way. Rose had a '90s look, buzzed hair, nice and jacked. Triceps were statuesque. Face was getting red, dangerously, like about to explode. "You want to wait in the back?" I said. The waiting room was hot and cranky. Some big guys were lurking, antsy, harshing the vibe. "Come on," I said and shouted an exam room number into the air, Monica caught it with an eyebrow.

They were already, by then, crying. Starting to really heave. I smacked the paper on the exam table like, get on up here, handed them a box of tissues.

"They'll be with you soon," I said. That made it actually worse.

I filled a plastic cup with tap water, held it out.

"I don't know if I should tell her," Rose said.

"OK," I said.

"I cheated on her," they said, and waved a hand at their torso and I got it.

"I get it," I said.

"It's like, once I lie about it I'll have to lie my whole life. I'll lie about a baby."

"It's OK," I said.

"It's not OK," they said.

"Cheating isn't the worst," I said. "It's like the most common thing."

"It's not OK," they said.

What are you supposed to say? The lights fluttered and I was still gripping the cup.

"I thought about telling her," they said. "I thought about asking her if she wanted to, like, have the baby together. But he'd have to be involved. Every time she saw him it would be like, I cheated."

"Not everyone is that boring," I said. "But I don't know her myself."

They said: "If she finds out I lied about something this big, she'll never forgive me."

I accidentally drank the water.

"How do people lie like that? How do they live with it?" they said.

Sometimes jobs get personal. "When it's better than telling the truth," I said.

"I bet you'll figure it out," I added.

"People must cry at you all day," they said.

"Water off a duck's back," I said. "Statistically"—and they flinched, like I was going to talk about the procedure—"statistically, I'm pretty sure most people cheat. Like, a majority. In my opinion people in general should be more chill about something most people do."

"I don't think it's OK," they said. "I don't think I'm going to be OK."

They pressed their hands hard against their eye sockets. In my experience this just makes you cry more, but I can't solve everything. They said: "Have you ever cheated?"

"Well," I paused for a sec, "I honestly don't know how to answer that. I mean, I don't necessarily have that kind of information? But sure."

Then I said, having thought about it: "Maybe I've only ever cheated."

I tried. I said: "Fucking isn't like totally one thing or totally another thing. It's always different things at the same time. That's why it's so confusing that it can like, flip a switch, pregnant. Like, on/off. What the hell. So I hear you."

"I just don't know what to do," they said.

"Yeah," I said. "Seems like you kinda don't. But here you are at the abortion clinic"—Monica cracked the door, lightly knocking—"so let's roll."

All that was true but I got talked to later. "Angela," Monica said, "you need to act like you care."

"I do care," I said. But caring was supposed to look some other way. My way didn't count.

How bout now?

I guess I won't run again. Ever?

I woke up with wet paper drooled onto my left cheek. Didn't know I was asleep. That must be what made me think of running.

When you're like a half hour into a run and you forget that's what you're doing. It's not a high. If you've literally ever been high you wouldn't call it that. But the space around the act of running vanishes. All the pressure to make yourself do it, to think about doing it, to get good at it, the effort that's the whole machine—about a half hour in something eases or vanishes. There you are. You're just doing it, without knowing more about it. Fucking is like this. Fucking can be like this. Not much else is. For everything else there's something in the way, you're in the way of the thing you're doing, the place where you want to be, which is the place where you vanish. It's not that I'm not thinking. But you can just think something dumb, like the theme song to *Free Willy*. You're running and singing to your-self and it's just the theme song to *Free Willy*. Not even a song anyone felt bad about getting rid of when people tried to get rid of everything Michael Jackson ever did, like they could magically erase like a lifetime of radio from our heads, anyway no one was like, NO! NOT THE THEME SONG TO *FREE WILLY*! But that's the sort of thing that takes over my brain. Just junk, like thoughts that don't mean anything, nothing's happening. You notice where your foot is coming down, you don't want to catch a divot, roll an ankle in the field. You lift your knees to power up this sledding hill, which right now in the spring is yellow with old grass, probably a thousand ticks birthing. You get up on your toes. Your thoughts are light and stupid. You can see through them. It's like you can catch the path light takes through seawater without hitting the shit plastic. Doesn't matter. A pressure, releasing. It's not like cumming, it's like not thinking about whether you'll cum.

I wonder if people will remember my championship. After this.

God I'm like some sad dad showing his kid his trophy, some figurine with a cheap guy-shape wearing shorts the wrong length for the next era. His kid's just thinking, did you really wear shorts like that, oh my god?

My aunt came to the big championship race, straight from work, still wearing her padded-shoulder blazer. She was standing in a weird spot on the course, where no one else would have thought to stand. My mom wasn't coming, so my aunt stepped up, made the effort. She looked really shocked when she saw me, I guess because I was in the front pack and had a face like a monster. I don't think she thought she'd see me out front like that, like there were four girls and then four hundred girls but I was one of the four. She was all by herself by the side of the trail, in the woods where no one was. I think she'd had some meeting then drove almost two hours, trotted to that weird spot, in her tight suit and white sneakers. I remember I glided over a big root then looked up and caught her full in the eye. She cheered like, *go Angela*. But then once she was behind me—we were heading downhill and into the third mile—all of a sudden she shrieked, horribly, smashing the trance sound of our breathing: *GO ANGELA!!!!!* It was so loud. But I think that really helped. Like, I cracked up. I thought, *oh my god*. It reminded me that I wasn't dying, this was just a race I could win.

Stupid if I told her all this.

The Michael Jackson thing, it's like, everyone knew, but they pretended not to know, but then once they couldn't pretend anymore they were *shocked*. How can you be shocked? We all totally knew this. We totally know fucked-up things like this happen and were probably, right here and now, happening. But it's like this every time, fake shock. Like anytime it turns out a rich guy raped 75 women, people are like, HE RAPED 75 WOMEN!?! and they tear their hair out and announce they'll catch him faster next time, they have to do better. And it's like yeah, 35 women told you about it already, but I guess the last 40 were a surprise?

I don't shock easy but people don't like that about me. People need to feel like they can surprise you.

It took a while but I'm starting to get that this is one of people's problems with me.

What I've been thinking (and I feel almost surprised about it) is that before—I mean, in the past—it seemed like the secret to running was to sink way into the middle, lose your awareness of anything else, and then to pull yourself back out. Like, you get into the zone, everything around the running itself has eased off. But the zone gets deeper as the run gets harder. Then, in the zone, in the deep part of it, you're like, *I'm dying*. Your thoughts are just *dying dying dying*. So then when your aunt suddenly appears, wearing nude stockings and extremely white sneakers, tucking her extremely bobbed hair behind her ear in the middle of the woods, and says louder than you've ever heard her say anything in the 17 years you've been alive

GO ANGELA!, you're like, I'm not dying, I'm just hurting, which is fine, that makes sense, if I hurt enough I can win. So you have to step back out of the zone. It's a rhythm, I guess. In it, then knowing about it. You have to forget, then remember.

But that was before. What makes this situation different is that I am actually, potentially, dying. Hunger strikes kill. So even though I thought all that state champ stuff was preparation for this, in fact this is something else. You have to go further in. You have to keep forgetting how to remember.

I called your journalist friend, my aunt says on the screen of my phone. *He'll call you 10 a.m. tomorrow.*

Thought I was done for the day. Bored? There's no TV or anything. On the last last day Donna turned off the internet, for some kind of security reason, like that would prevent anything, but she decided it would, she made a lot of announcements. I could use my mobile data but that adds up. I guess if I don't make it through this, it won't matter about my mobile data. But if I do make it, I don't want to have a $400 bill. Seeing as I am unemployed. So I'm trying to hold out, just a little scrolling here and there, look a couple things up when I think of them. Now that I'm here at work and messed up I keep remembering things. Like, things from work, from the bottom of the laundry basket of the brain.

Without the internet do we just remember things?

Just now I was standing in front of the back supply closet deciding if I could lift one of those huge water cooler jug things (there's still two in there and I kind of want one, I want to fill cups at the cooler, use the blue lever) and I remembered I'd done exactly this maybe four years ago. It was me and a girl who used to work here. I would say I've forgotten her name but did I ever know it? Something like . . . Priscilla. She was getting a *master's in public health*. She said that a lot. Good for you. "Do you think we can carry one of these?" she was asking me as we looked at the water cooler jugs. "I doubt it," I said, but we did try, it basically worked but Monica freaked out and started helping. Priscilla had asked me something about college or grad school. Like the internship program she was in, she thought I was in that too. "I didn't go to college," I said. "I started but then I got arrested and had to do jail and probation stuff for a while."

"I'm sorry," she said. "That sounds really hard."

"Well," I said, "it wasn't unexpected because I was selling drugs and I sucked at it."

She said something about legalizing weed. I bet she got every A.

"Absolutely," I said, "but I'm talking about pills. I mean, I wasn't that into pills myself, it was just a business situation. Just like, I wasn't that into abortions, I just got a job here."

I added: "I'm more into them now. Abortions, I mean."

Who cares what she said, a few months later Priscilla was gone—she'd said she wanted to run her own clinic but that was before everything got overturned, everything heated up, before laws started switching up, like there could be a new law every day, you would call this huge list of patients to tell them whatever, then some new bullshit, some judge did or didn't block something, the phones were ringing and the clock was ticking, like some supreme clock somewhere or every little clock everywhere, I was getting a feeling like everyone's personal biological clock was in me, like that kids' movie where a crocodile swallowed an alarm clock and he's coming for you. Like sometimes in the middle of work I'd look up at something normal, like one of Krys's sunset photos, the one where there's a little bird crossing the big circle of sun, and it wouldn't mean anything, you couldn't trust things to just mean something normal anymore. Sitting there at the desk, everyone running around but also not doing the one thing that would matter, I don't know how to describe it. But I think that's why Dr. M lost her shit. And the death threats. More and more death threats. And Priscilla, I was thinking, Priscilla and all those well-meaning gals stuck in the past, it's not like there was a place they could get away from it all, because Krys was saying even in like New York things were crazy with the overflow from everywhere else, pregnant mobs calling in, flying in . . . But of course you could still get away from it, if you wanted. You could tell yourself you needed a better job, just to pay off your loans and not get shot and not get too stressed out while you tried to start a family yourself, with some on-brand husband like Priscilla probably had, and you'd go help deliver babies or run a nice program in a nice hospital in the suburbs and forget your little dream of being an abortion doc at some inner-city strip-mall joint like ours.

Where jailbirds like me hid your travel mug sometimes (a lot) just because we were bored and thought you were boring.

And a few months after Priscilla left, the whole jail thing came up again, now that I'm remembering the order of things. Three elders from the city's big foundation were visiting. Donna had been drilling us for weeks. The place looked shiny, almost wet. I wasn't involved, other than being lectured for a week beforehand about my outfit choices. I did look good that day— *you look nice,* Krystal said aggressively. Toward the end of my shift I was taking a dead lightbulb to the dead lightbulb place and I heard an older woman in the hallway, wearing a blue scarf, blue stone sparkling in her rich ear, say to Donna how "the foundation also appreciates how you hire staff with criminal records, which coincides with our commitment to supporting reentry and rehabilitation." And she glanced at Monica, who was just then heading up front, through the door at the end of the hallway.

"It's me actually," I said, from behind them.

"Ah hello, Angela," Donna said.

"Don't worry," I said, "they don't let me near the good drugs."

The woman shifted her little look from Monica to me and extended her hand. "So nice to meet you—"

"Turns out," I said, "white girls can get arrested too, if they really put in the work."

"Oh," the woman said, "please don't think I assumed—"

Blah blah we all knew she'd assumed. She'd met a couple staff members, one was Black, and she'd assumed. If I didn't already know I was right, the way she'd denied it sealed the deal. She wasn't *surprised*. (Though to be fair, I was arrested out in the country, more of a white scenario.) If she didn't know what I was talking about—if she wasn't thinking of anyone in particular, wasn't looking particularly at anyone, was just mentioning something she'd read somewhere—she'd have looked confused when I said what I said. But no, she was smooth as hell, just extended her hand. So I knew. And Monica knew. Monica who was definitely (like I said, it's a short hallway) in earshot and who said, when I reappeared up front, "Angela, anyone ever tell you you're like a broken clock?"

Right before I left to get the bus—Dr. M and these scented donors were going to an important dinner—Dr. M pulled me aside as I was coming out of the bathroom, pulled me by the wrist right into exam room 3. She put her petite self in front of the closed door, like, you're trapped in here, but this won't take long.

She said: "The grant that foundation could give us would help hundreds of women receive the care they need. Most of these women will not look like you and will not have been born having your advantages. You think you scored a point today. But for other people this is not a game. Angela, you will shut your mouth. My impression is they would not like it if I fired you for this incident. But you should know that from this day on," she tipped my chin up with her soft steady finger, so she could look right at me, "in my heart you are fired."

So who'll get the last word?

Do you think they took the grant back, after? What'll they do with all that money, now that there's no one to help those *hundreds of women*, or the hundreds after them, or after them, forever . . . Turns out Dr. M got fired first. Didn't see that coming. Turns out this was just another day before the end of the world.

Day 6

Talked to you this morning.
Staying hydrated.

Day 7

The thing I fucking hate is you'll see I didn't write yesterday and think that's about you.

I was hungry. I lay around and thought about food.

I keep trying to get comfy on the baby fake-leather couch in Dr. M's office but it's too short, so your neck hurts, and the not-leather stick-smacks to your skin.

I'm not getting any good religious feelings.

I have a headache like way deep in the middle of my shoulders. It's in the roots of my teeth. Like a needle piercing up through the base of each tooth. Fuck.

Yesterday I was trying to remember every half-stack of Pringles I've ever eaten. Didn't I, one time, balance a joint, still smoking, on the mythical curve of a Pringle?

Then I was thinking, I could get a job sorting the big crunchy nuggets out of boxes of cereal, separate them out from the flakes, make a supercereal. I don't see the point of the flakes. I don't see the point of that flakey ratio.

How are you, Angela? you said, which was stupid.

I'm on a hunger strike?

And by the end of the convo it still wasn't clear if you'd help, if you'd write a story.

If we write a story people will know you're in there, you said. *The cops will come.*

Publicity will protect me though.

Ange do you even read the paper I write for? Where ads for colon cleansers pop up after every sentence and every article is only like 6 sentences long? I don't write for the New York Times.

You should, I said. I meant it nice.

Talk to my mom. She agrees with you. Actually don't talk to my mom. She was not a fan of us dating. And she's not an abortion person. Like MAYBE in the case of rape or incest.

Well we do those cases too, I said. *We did.*

I'll see what I can do.

Hey me too, I'm seeing what I can do.

Angela are you OK?

You used the phrase *cry for help* like you'd just learned it.

Ever think of Rose who had some kind of costume exploding out of her bag, like puffy cheap medieval-looking, thick wad of skirts, and I never learned if she was like some for-real Shakespearean actor or a Ren Fair LARPer, she had the bag on her lap, then put it on the floor carefully, got up and crossed the waiting room to ask me, "Do you know how much longer it'll be?"

"Sorry"—she said right away, before I'd said anything, did my face like yell at her? We were booked solid and part-time Stevie had got her days mixed up—"I don't mean I'm like in a rush, like I can't wait to get it out, maybe that question seems like a cry for help or something . . ."

"No, it's our bad," I said, "one of our nurses is late" (Krystal gave me a look like who was I . . .), "it's totally normal that you don't want to sit in this amazing waiting room all afternoon." Rose actually smiled, like that was the result I wanted, I guess. "I just have to be somewhere later," she said, and I was about to point out that she might not be in shape to get herself there but then I thought, if people want to work or play a little bleed-y and woozy, lend a little authenticity to their Medieval Times, I should judge not lest I be, etc. "Hang in there," I said, "the night is young."

John, now you're like, "when we were dating"? 8 a.m. some Saturday morning there was a knock on the door of your apartment. "Fuck fuck fuck fuck fuck"—this was all you, I was waiting to see if I cared. You were supposed to go to a family thing. A cousin's wedding? You had to take a ferry. "We'll miss the ferry," your mom was saying in the kitchen. She started in on the dishes, making a show out of it. "John, you shouldn't be living in filth. You have company," and she nodded at me. I was standing in the bedroom doorway wearing your White Stripes T-shirt and no pants. You kept passing by me like I was in the way.

"Half of those are his roommate's," I said.

"It doesn't matter whose they are," your mom said.

I knew she was a teacher, because you'd said so and because anyone could tell. I didn't want to move and I didn't want to get dressed. I liked the smell of your shirt and I liked how my legs looked. I wanted to sleep in your bed when you weren't there.

You thought I was leaving right after you but I didn't. Not until that night. I finished washing the dishes because I thought you'd think that was funny, though later I realized it didn't matter, your roommate messed the whole place up again before you got back. I didn't see your mom again. You hadn't invited me to whatever this wedding was even though we'd been fucking for months or actually, think about it now, years. I've never even seen a ferry. Like in real life. I mean, I understand the concept. So we were dating?

No way could I describe how long the days are in here.

No, it's the nights.

Even though the front windows are boarded up (and those are the main windows, this place is a real cave), while it's light out I feel like, OK, I'm on some kind of sick vacation. It's daytime but hey I'm not working. I don't have shit to do. I've been setting up the waiting room chairs and tables, walking patterns around them, lots of figure 8s. But a person needs, like, dinnertime. I'm not even that into things like that—I like to eat out of a Tupperware, leaning against the fridge, looking out my window at my neighbor's TV, the blank backs of their heads. But without something defining that twilight moment, there's just these empty hours, when I feel like I'll puke, my head pounds, and every minute takes like ten minutes to pass. I hate it. Like 7 to 9. More like 6 to 10. And things are rumbling, too loud to ignore. The gut noise is disgusting. Probably the roaches are like, what *is* that? And I haven't stopped shitting yet. That's not over for me yet. It's dramatic.

Those are the exact hours I hated dating. If anything was ever dating. 7 to 9. 6 to 10? I like happy hour. I don't like the part that's like, let's make dinner, here we are cuddling on the couch. Here we are watching two episodes of the same show every night. Shows are fine, shows are great. But I don't like fucking anyone I know I'm going to fuck. I need the suspense. I want the suspense. Suspense isn't the word. I need to feel like, right up to the moment it's happening, I'm not sure it'll happen. Like, you didn't want to want it. But then you had to admit, yeah you wanted it. I actually love texting when I don't know if someone will text me back. Later you can see if you care, how much did you want it. I would say the day I met your mom—who apparently thought we were dating—that was the beginning of the end of us ever having been dating. If we ever were, then we weren't. I would have gone to the wedding if you asked, but only if I didn't expect you to ask. If I expected it, I wouldn't have wanted it. It could have been like a fun thing. You: a person with a cousin who sends invitations in the literal mail, a person wearing a sports coat on the deck of a ferry. And me: tucking your White Stripes shirt into a skirt and having the shortest possible conversations with the fewest members of your family. Rubbing one hand against you through your slacks while we listened to seagulls or whatever. But you missed the whole point. When you got back I realized you thought I was upset like someone who wanted to be your girlfriend and didn't get to go on a boring official trip. I was upset like someone who didn't want to be your girlfriend but who could have been hot and rude on this boring outing, saving everyone from the whole situation, especially your dick. But no, you didn't seem to get that this was an option. That's kind of my option, like the whole point of me. A lot of guys get that about me, and these are dumber meaner guys. You were always treating me like I was just bad at being boring.

Like that time you fucked me in the bathroom stall and I hooked my shirt for a sec on the coat hook on the door and waved my arms around. It was funny, a joke, haha. You paused and said *are you OK?* You said *we can go back to my place.* But you were too hard to go anywhere. Am I OK? I'm fucking you in this public bathroom. I'm amazing. Are *you* OK? You wasted so much time apologizing totally insincerely for not being the good boyfriend you should have known I didn't want. But think about it—*that* was hot. I was always waiting for you to figure this basic thing out about who I was and it was hot that you totally couldn't. You always underestimated me but the fact that you didn't understand that I understood that was this suspense that kept building. It kept me interested and probably interesting. He'll figure it out, I'd think. He'll get that the thing with the hook was just a joke. That I can jerk off while listening to him talk to his mom about his roommate's crusty dishes.

But you never got it.

Yesterday you were like, *I don't get it, I didn't think you even liked your boss.*

Why can't you see. Liking is easy. I don't care about liking. It's not enough to want something, that's easy. You have to be scared to want it. You can't just make dinner.

Evening again. Witching hour. I've been in this sleeping bag all afternoon. Exam room 2, which I think might be the worst. Shiver shiver. Really sweating it up in here. The whole sweating-while-cold thing has never made sense to me, but the proof is in because this sleeping bag reeks. Earlier I tried to hop my way to refill my water bottle. Little lemon, little salt. Honestly I thought about it for a long time before getting up. Getting up is an event. You have to kind of prop up slowly, in stages. Head rush, shivering. Big cramps.

Does anyone know when their last shit has been taken?

I have the water with me now but I feel pretty bad. My fault for trying to hop my way in a sleeping bag. But I was freezing. And when I got myself upright my own blood just didn't participate. All the blood just dove for my feet and my head was a big bloodfree balloon. Like there was no difference between an actual skull skin blood organ situation that stood five foot five and the old poster on the wall behind me, a portrait of a bisected girl, pretty teensy curl of fallopian tube, featureless face, general white-person flesh look. We were the same, poster girl and I. Gone 2D. I clipped my arm hard on the counter as I went down. Hit the corner. Must have been trying to catch myself. I think my arm was tucked awkward inside the bag and so I flung it out while I pirouetted down, like a helicopter spinning down from a maple tree, but dumber. My arm is still kind of bleeding. The blood is weird. I can't tell if it's weird. There's a dent, like the counter stuck a sharp tiny finger into the flesh and curled it up, like *come here*. Anyway that's why there's blood all over this.

Yesterday I dragged two exam tables together, it was not easy, and now exam room 1 has no table and there are two here in room 2, which I think was the wrong choice, something's wrong with this room, but I'm not going to drag everything back. I laid some binders out to make a hard surface on the second table. Now I can prop myself up, lean over and write.

John, you owe me this. I'm like in your world now, I'm news. I'm obviously interesting.

For this to work I need to be news.

It's not a hunger strike if no one knows about it. That's just a diet.

Here I am in some shut-down office, dieting.

What did Janine say to me once?

"I used to be like you."

Bullshit and she knew it. Janine was a Donna. Donnas know Donnas. They'd kick me out of that convention on sight. Honestly if I have an equivalent on the other side, it's the old drunk guy who still turns up in the parking lot every few months, like he didn't get the memo, no one told him his kind got reformed out, and he's holding some wet Bible he keeps trying to stuff in his back pocket, where it doesn't fit, but he keeps trying, like he's still thinking, even though he owns probably just the one Bible and the one pair of pants, *get in there* . . . That's me. Whenever he comes Janine smiles real tight, and I once saw her reach forward and—like he was one of her little sons—zip his jacket up over his dumbass shirt, which bore variously gendered stick figures angrily arranged around some math symbols, as if this was how a higher being would communicate their "law." Janine's smile is 100% unconvincing. I used to think this was a weakness. She's obviously never smiling, it's just something her face does to keep men calm. But recently—maybe just now—I realized that deep down guys know it's not real and that's what they like. She's the girl next door, but she's a killer. She's a sleeper agent, she's on their side.

When Janine fake-smiled at you, you thought, oh yeah, what if I barely pretended to live in the world. What if I kept my dead eyes on my own mission.

"I used to be like you."

She said it twice. I didn't respond the first time so she said it again. I was just then doing something a little obnoxious. I was handing out condoms to the protestors. Fruity condoms.

Not handing out. Throwing at. We got samples from a manu-
facturer. They showed up in the mail and I'd take some of the
fun ones home. John, jog your memory? But that day the protestors were too fucking much. They were staying on the island
in the parking lot, sure, but goddamn. The whiny hoses of
their throats were emptying onto every normal person walking
up, someone just wanting a little basic help with the wildest
part of being alive. How life makes more of itself, it just uses
you, like you're not part of it. It's normal to have some questions about that, push back. But these whiners. And let's not
pretend women's voices don't suck. It was like a sorority had
spent 20 years braiding each other's hair too tight while
driving up the costs of each other's weddings. Personally I was
done. I was hungover, I think, and they were slamming their
rubber baby dolls into my sweet young brainstem till whisky
oozed out. I got a big handful of grape- and strawberry-flavored
condoms out of my bag and ran out there. "Contraceptives for
the community!" I screamed. I aimed for Janine's mouth.
That's when she said it.

"I used to be like you."

I was staring. You could say I looked insane but I was the
one getting paid for my time. Right then what I was thinking—
she was wearing a yellow-checked Talbots-type sundress that
was kind of like a summer turtleneck—was that Janine had a
huge rack, and so we were nothing alike. You're either a boob
girl or you're not. If you're not, you're probably a leg girl.
I don't mean people can't make a change if they want, they

should do what they feel. I mean people know, moment by moment, which they are. It's a deep feeling. Janine's boobs were her whole point of view. I was braless. Whenever I threw a fruity condom at her face my nipple skimmed the inside of my shirt like a mean giggle.

"Fuck you, Janine," I said.

"I was standing right where you're standing right now," she said. "I worked for the other side. I helped kill so many babies. I feel your pain."

I was getting the feeling this was a new speech even to her obedient compadres. Like, people stopped to listen. Was I real or were they?

"We don't kill babies here," I said. "So if you were killing babies somewhere, that seems like more of a personal problem."

"I can hear your pain," Janine said. "You're feeling their pain, and your own pain as a woman, and it's filling you with anger. That's what you'll understand when you join the side of life. You can love and serve God's creation instead of destroying the most innocent among us. Trust me. I'm not angry anymore."

She'd stepped forward and I could see blobs in her mascara. Don't do the bottom lashes, Janine.

"Eight fucking feet," I said.

"You're not a patron," she said. "That law is for patrons."

"Angela"—Donna was saying, hot hand on my throwing arm—"we need you inside."

Janine and I could have gone some more rounds but here was Rose, walking slowly from an old station wagon toward the clinic door, and the whole dance was starting, the pamphlets, shrieking, simpering little pleas.

Janine, own it, you're the angriest bitch I know.

John, what I'm saying is, that's why I DM'ed her.

Janine gets it, you don't.

Day 9

I didn't know my aunt would come too. She got out of her car. She walked right up to Janine to introduce herself. These are her instincts. I was standing in the doorway.

This was yesterday. It was a pretty full day so I didn't get a chance to write.

The windows are still—if you'd come, I wouldn't have to tell you—boarded up, sheets of plywood. (I think part-time Stevie, who also works for some private practice, and so maybe was calmer because she'd only lost half a job, got her boyfriend to do this. Donna was saying something about it on that last last day, yanking chairs back from the front windows with insane energy.) The plywood's been tagged. On the right, it's just neighborhood kids or whatever, nothing impressive, though I'm glad they're like getting outside and not just online all day. On the left: **MURDERERS**. Was this Janine's handwriting? Not neat enough. But she probably tags with her nondominant hand, she's sly. Janine was standing in the street, not on the sidewalk, wearing a creepy peacoat. "You can come closer," I said, "we're closed." Janine held up her phone, took a photo. I tried to look saintly. I had on a wrinkly white shift dress over a black long-sleeved shirt. I'd had to add the shirt unfortunately because my arm was so bruised and trickling. "Hello," my aunt said to Janine—before she even said hi to me, like Janine was hosting this party—shaking hands, stating her full name and that she was on city council. If asked she'd have named some committees. "Are you a friend"—she asked Janine, eyeing me—"of Angela's?"

"Yes," Janine said.

"Welcome," I said. I kept one hand hard on the doorframe to stay upright. God, food is important.

Smell of Jamaican takeout from the place across the parking lot, on the far side of the strip's two vacant storefronts. I had to swallow a goblet of spit to say:

"Thank you both so much for coming."

My aunt took a tiny step forward. Was she *scared*?

"Angela, you need to come home with me right now. I know you're upset, you're right to be upset, but this isn't helping. I think we can all agree"—and she spread her hands wide, including Janine—"this isn't an effective way to get your point across."

Janine was noncommittal. She lifted a hand to her hair and I realized it was raining.

I didn't invite them in.

"I'm not trespassing," I said to my aunt. "I mean, it's a gray area. Dr. M's son or Donna would have to complain."

Janine turned her phone horizontal to get the whole word: **MURDERERS**. Thank god I'd wiped off my red lipstick, which had looked too undead.

"Angela?" she said. (Did she not know my name? What did she call us, to herself?) "Your name is Angela?"

My aunt looked at her suspiciously. I think there were exactly eight feet between them, like Janine just went through life this way.

"Angela," Janine said. "You led me to believe there was a protest underway to try to"—she looked around, pulsing bass from a passing car, the almost empty lot—"reopen the clinic and free the imprisoned abortionist. Is this what I'm looking at?"

(My aunt tried: "Angela, who—")

"Yes," I said. "I'm on a hunger strike. This is the eighth day of my hunger strike to protest the false imprisonment of Dr. M."

"Well, it's not *false* imprisonment," my aunt said.

"Oh my god," I said. "She was doing her fucking job."

"Her job was murder," Janine said, gesturing at the plywood like it was evidence.

"I am going to continue my hunger strike until she's released," I announced into the wet underwhelming air.

"Angela," said my aunt.

Janine put her phone in her coat pocket, like she was leaving.

"Don't you want to save a life?" I asked Janine, shimmying a little, like I meant *me*, ta-da.

I remember thinking: her face is like a Terminator's. Like she's made of that alien steel from the future, housing her preprogrammed soul. 100% relentless. But even then I thought, honestly, she's more like Sarah Connor. She looks like she does pull-ups and lands zingers all day, prioritizes a very important baby boy. She looks like she's looking right at an establishment she personally got boarded up and shut down, and she feels great.

"You belong to a culture of death," Janine said. "All this"—she waved her hand, somehow also including the wig store, the sad chiropractor—"extends from a failure to value God's gift of life."

I guess the point of those movies is that Sarah Connor, mom of the future messiah, herself becomes a sort of Terminator. But still vulnerable, which makes her human and hot. She's as relentless in her intent to protect her son and the future of humanity as the machines are when programmed to kill. To defeat machines as smart as people, people have to be as single-minded as machines. Or as mothers. Single-minded about freedom, ironic. *No fate.* What I'm saying is, I remembered Janine lacked the power of irony. She ran on loser fuel.

I sat down in the doorway. The result was not modest. There was a little blood smudge below my palm. My aunt took a baby step closer.

"Janine, what do you tell the kids?" I asked. "What do you tell the young girls who've been raped and impregnated by their dad or their uncle?"

"That they don't have to suffer more harm. They don't have to harm themselves and their child, their suffering is over now. God's love will—"

"*This* is God's love," I shouted, waving my arms, it was awkward, I was seated, kind of balled up and flailing.

("Angela—")

Janine didn't blink: "The doctor wasn't convicted for helping victims of rape and incest. You know that. She broke the law. She violated the rules of her own profession."

A raindrop hit the bone that bumps up from my right foot, the bone that always rubs in sneakers. I swear even that bone was sticking out more, like my feet were slimming down. Why was I wearing flip-flops? It's October.

I think I said: "You don't get to choose. You don't get to say, oh, this kid was raped, this fetus has bad enough defects, we all agree, but this baby could live a little while, this woman, she could have left him before it happened, she could have moved back home instead of staying, or gotten to the pharmacy before work even if she got fired for being late, or she could have gotten out of the car and run home. She could have taken the pill every day at exactly 7 a.m. instead of hitting snooze. She could have stopped drinking even though she didn't know yet. She could've never ever drunk. She could've not worried about her job and just gotten pregnant two years earlier when the odds were better. She could've double-checked to see if he was wearing a condom like he said, like she saw him put on. No. You don't get to choose. Think about it. A priest doesn't choose who shows up every Sunday. You don't get to be like, oh, when I said sinners I meant the really good ones, like the ones who aren't sinners."

"Angela," my aunt said, "there are more effective—"

"There were heartbeats," Janine said. "She knew there were heartbeats."

"They're not *heartbeats*," I said, "but yeah, she knew. She did exactly what the law said not to do, you got her on that."

"I think we should have higher standards," Janine said. "I think medicine shouldn't hurt the most vulnerable among us. We can do better, for women and for all our children. I think it's worth considering how your standards got so low."

(My aunt's face didn't love that.)

"I think," I said to Janine, "you should live in the real world where real people have to live. Not some made-up world where you pretend that everything that ever happens is because people didn't follow your made-up rules."

"And are you living in the real world," Janine said—hands out of her pockets, cream-pink nails in the gray rain—"right now?"

Fuck.

"You said you'd help me," I said to my aunt. I didn't think before saying it. I guess that's how talking usually goes for me. "You said you'd help me."

She'd said that twice. Not recently. Once when my mom died. And once, way more reluctantly, when I was on probation, figuring shit out. Pretty sure I got this job because she put in a word with a friend of Donna's, in a reality in which Donna has friends.

"I am helping," my aunt said. "I'm trying to help. Please come with me, get in the car, Angela."

"You're the same," I said. "You two have the exact same problem. You know, when people ask you for help, you're supposed to give them the help they're asking for. If you give them some other help you think is better for them, you're an asshole."

"She was good at her job," I added. "Dr. M is good at her job."

"It's more than a job," I said, but that still didn't get at it.

Did Janine really say *I'll pray for you*?

That's what I remember. But I was tuckered out.

"You have to let a doctor come see you," my aunt said. "Please."

"Whatever," I said. "This is literally a doctor's office."

In Janine's photo I look like a very old child. Does she have some filter designed for her enemies? Wondering if I didn't look my best before I started the starvation thing. But the point is, late afternoon yesterday she posted it on her social media. Saying there's no tactic we won't use, etc., etc., etc., further proof... And I do look pretty psychotic. Well I bet Jesus looked like shit on the cross. John, why am I even bothering, because two reporters who weren't you just came by. They, like, knocked. One of them looked like a really smart 16-year-old (she works for the alt-weekly, she says, though I don't get the impression this is a paying position) and the other one said she was an old classmate of my aunt's. She did not say friend. "This is the ninth day of my hunger strike," I said. "I want them to release Dr. M. She can't hunger strike because of her diabetes."

And then, just like an hour ago, the phone rang. It was 8 p.m., maybe. I answered like always, "Patients First Health Clinic, this is Angela," then added, "we're technically closed."

"Angela?"

"Yes?" I said.

"It's Donna. You're really there?"

"Yes," I said. "Hi, Donna."

Donna had seen Janine's post. She asked a lot of questions.

"Angela," Donna said, "you're crazy. OK. I'm going to make sure it's known that you're allowed to be there. Do you need anything?"

"Not really," I said. "I'm low-maintenance."

She hmm'ed for a minute. She said: "We need more press." Then she said: "Your aunt called me, you know."

"OK," I said.

"She's worried," Donna said. "Family always worries."

"You're not worried?"

She took a beat. Donna's always on top of everything but she never rushes. How does that work?

"Worried isn't the word for it," she said. "I didn't think things would go the way they went. I thought I would be ready, but I wasn't ready. I'd say, Angela, that I had a dark night of the soul.

But you were ready, weren't you. You're a girl who's prepared for bad news."

"I guess so."

"I appreciate that," she said. "I'm going to call you tomorrow. We're going to send some people around to help out."

She didn't say who we or they were. Guess I'll see. I picture Donna with an old-school Rolodex in which everyone she's ever met is sorted and cross-referenced by skill set. *Knife fights. FileMaker Pro.*

She hung up.

Is Donna on Team Suicide?

Day 10

Saw what your friend wrote, based on our convo. Under the headline **PUBLICITY STUNT**. He sure used the verb *claim*. And why that photo of Dr. M, all handcuffed and defendant-looking, head bowed behind the bad table. Gray roots, skunked out. You're right, your paper is trash. Sorry. But I had to scroll way down to see anything about anything, the first 4 minutes of scroll are all advice columns run by the kids of dead advice columnists, ads for the one house in this city that costs $1 million, a feature on a guy who was on the baseball team when they were good 10 years ago, then interviews with some fans just like remembering, 5 articles on cops who may or may not get put on leave, an article on how much people love this new towpath, a photo of a kid who got his eye shot out at a protest against police brutality, an interview with the quarterback from the '80s discussing rape-y rumors about the new quarterback, 2 hotels going bankrupt and what readers could personally do, a review of a new Taco Bell product, maybe 15 articles on high school sports and only 1 girls' team and it's gymnastics, an article on a bill to keep trans girls off girls' sports teams, I guess if you just switch up which girls you treat the shittiest that fools some people (and now everyone has an excuse to check out kids' genitals, I guess), then an article on some politicians who aren't fans of China, some celebrities' 46th birthdays, an article about an actress in a Transformers movie a few plastic surgeries ago who I guess is making changes in her dating life, an incorrect list of the 10 best Nine Inch Nails albums, and then . . . **PUBLICITY STUNT**.

I got your text with a link to the article like an hour after I'd already found it. You said, *I can't write about u bc of our relationship but this is my coworker. Ange ur not really gonna keep on w this? DANGEROUS*

I texted back: *u think I didnt have a "relationship" w your coworker?*

Buzz buzz buzz.

I'm lying down.

Don't know if anyone at your paper does research, but Janine's social media is a treasure trove. Follow your finger down down down and there she is on the podium with that state senator, total fucking Nazi, standing beside him with little sparkles in her eyes. Holding a pair of oversized scissors. It's a ribbon-cutting for one of those crisis pregnancy centers, Valley Women's Care Center—like, sweetie, we've got you nestled here in some cozy valley, not surrounded by soybean fields and pig slaughterhouses like you think. I think Janine's kids are there, or at least there's three boys with her jawline, sporting sharp little khaki pants and polos. The Nazi rests his hand on one boy's shoulder. A few years back the Nazi went in hard on defending a wrestling coach at the state school who it turned out really was molesting high school kids in his "recruiting program." Some people come back from that—the boys the coach got to—but some don't. I think if you stepped back later and looked at their whole lives, you'd be like, no, they never quite came back. But you don't ever hear about what happens after, unless a suicide or overdose turns up in the news. Boys and girls, Janine is not looking out for you.

.

Pregnant women and girls, the article said, *seeking abortions after a fetal heartbeat can be detected, at approximately six weeks, now need to travel out of state* . . . *Pregnant women and girls* . . . Like hey trans men are running for that border too. You'd think the other side would brag about everyone they were fucking over. But then they'd have to admit everyone exists and is, like, a human who is alive. This was a Priscilla thing too (not her name?) now that I think about it. When she got trained in to say like *people* and *patients* and *you*, to not assume pronouns and stuff, she was like "I don't like to erase women from the conversation."

"Just say women and people, then," I said, "that'll cover it," like I was solving her problem.

"Especially at a place like this," she said, "I just really believe in centering women." What? This building was so full of women, everywhere you turned there was another one, making sure to tell you *god you're so skinny* like it wasn't a compliment or trying to diagnose how hungover you were.

I tried something like: "Listen, just be chill, honestly no one cares what you believe."

(Did I go to high school with Priscilla? Is that it? This bitch is so familiar. I'm thinking that's why she asked me so many questions, maybe we knew each other? Like she maybe dated this guy Robin, little birdname guy I made out with in the social studies closet?)

Krys used to remind me about vocab stuff, like I was some hick who couldn't handle it if a man walked in here pregnant, would have to crank my jaw back up off the floor like a cartoon. I did not need reminding but you can't win those fights. To Krys I was a hick and if I went to tell her why I actually, in some matters, was not, then I'd just be an angry hick. No one respects you because you tell them they should respect you. That has never worked throughout history. Didn't work on Priscilla either. Wherever she is now, I'm sure she's on her same bullshit, crying about how saying *they* must be what lost us everything and ended abortion. I swear, either Janine runs some sleeper cells or she doesn't even need to, women (centered!) are that dumb on their own.

Publicity stunt. Last time I heard that phrase was from the guy who did or did not have a gun. It was intern Allie's last day though we didn't know that yet. The waiting room was normal, except someone was eating, I'm serious, a container of diced onions. I mean, they had a separate dish they were sprinkling the onions on. But that meant they opened up, more than once, this container of pure onions. Is that what set everything off? I'm trying to see if the smell has gotten more appetizing—like my memory of the smell—in my current condition. Nope. Good sign. Guy walked in, sat down by onion lady, then got up and moved. So there didn't seem to be anything wrong with him. I was on hold in an insurance vortex. (You know, everyone forgets but there were certain calls Donna assigned to me specially. I can get past the first denial, wait out any 40-minute hold, no one outlasts me, that shit takes real persistence, you have to slog like a maniac through the first 3 operators until you get a supervisor, or one of the insurance co.'s "doctors," and then you can get something done.) Anyway, that day I was watching this guy in the waiting room tap his foot very hard, his knee was like one of those sun-powered dancing toys, my aunt has a little pumpkin-head in her kitchen window, bounce bounce bounce. Then he got up. He ran at me. Like he ran across the waiting room, fast around the people and chairs. I was behind the sliding glass window thing, closed. The glass either slows or stops bullets. Does it slow or stop bullets? The guy stopped right in front of me. With my finger I hung up the phone. I don't remember what I said. I looked at what I first thought was a hair stuck to the glass between us, making a line that ran down his face. But then I realized that the line was part of him, like a muscle tweaked by some expression he made, an acne or knife scar, I don't know. He was pale and his eyes looked wrong, like an ancient mask of eyes he was forced to wear. His sweatshirt was wadded up on one side and he was gripping the wad of it. "You bring her back out here," he said. "I have a gun. Before they do it to her. I have a gun."

I don't think I did or said anything. I was thinking. I was thinking I should find out her name, then say she wasn't here. There seemed to be some problems with that plan. I sensed the presence of problems. I was getting the receiver out from under my ear with the wrong hand. I think I said: *Sir, are you looking for someone?* Probably the most polite I've ever been honestly. I guess this was one time I truly cared what someone thought.

But then Donna was already out there. She has secret passages, like in *Clue*. Boom, conservatory, boom, waiting room. "No you don't," she said to the guy. "No you don't." She got louder and her hands were up in front of her, between her and him, like she was both surrendering and about to shove him down. Her palms were flat, hands wide, he could have palm-read her whole vacationless life. "No you don't," she said. "No."

Everyone in the waiting room was like a statue of a person in a nightmare. The onions were extreme. Donna's voice was the only thing in my head—like I could feel her voice in my mouth. She was backing him toward the door. There are two doors, of course, for security. There's an area in between, like closed in. Buzz him out, I thought, and I hit the buzzer. I could see the lines of Donna's bra under her red clingy shirt.

Her nails were a clashing pink. She was loud, she was endless. Her boobs, her belly, were our front line of defense. *No*, she was saying, and she kept stepping toward him, he kept stepping back. The sweatshirt was still wadded up, but his grip on it looked changed. Good sign? Buzz him out, I thought, and I was also dialing 911, phone off the hook, I could hear a low squeak from it. *NO YOU DON'T.* He was out. She was shutting the door in his face and I saw him, everyone saw him, step over in front of the left window and puke. Once quickly, then with a big heave, sinking on his knees into the puddle, again. It was orange, chunky, too red. I'd buzzed Donna back in. I hadn't thought about it. I'd just buzzed her on back. I picked up the phone and the 911 dispatcher was telling me where I was. "Yes, that's the address," I said. "He's a young white guy, with a weird face, puking outside, get here already."

"Good job," Donna said to me, nodding. I didn't say anything because puke was filling my whole head. Through the window I could still see the line of it, long from his foul mouth hole, gut to lip to pavement.

I walked pretty normal to the back, got it all up and out, wiped the toilet down real nice after. Things were going on. Through the window to the cops you could hear the guy saying "just a publicity stunt. Publicity stunt." I was watching Donna watch the cops. She talked with a nearly blank face. The day ended at a surprisingly usual time.

Someone said, "They said it wasn't a gun or it wasn't loaded?"

Someone said, "It was loaded."

I thought about it and then I executed: I bought like 30 Bailey's minis and spelled out *THX* on Donna's desk. I'd heard her say once she liked an Irish coffee before bed. I'd heard her say "I don't wait for cops." I got in very early to set all this up and my arrival time really turned heads. Later from my desk I heard her chuckle.

Not one mini bottle in the trash. Willpower.

Your friend's not as useless as I thought. There's more to the article, below a huge ad for some kind of laser-pointer bikini-waxing device.

Judge Russo, who presided over the criminal case, declined to comment.

Reached by phone, the office of the prosecutor stated: "The defendant was found guilty by a jury of her peers and was sentenced according to state law. Like everyone she is entitled to appeal. We do not overturn the laws of our society based on random acts of terrorism."

Rando terrorist! ☺ I've been called a lot but not that.

What I want is a big piece of white bread, the crusty kind, from a loaf you pull at with your hands, scales of crust splitting and falling, and then you spread that fake butter from a plastic tub all over a big piece like in a commercial for WASP lifestyles, grab a spoon and sprinkle, messy so it falls all over the plate, hot chocolate powder thick on top of the fake butter. If it's the kind with those tiny crystallized marshmallows, you'll find them later in your back teeth. Goddamn.

Evening now, like always, but this afternoon the doctor came. She had one of those leather bags doctors have in TV shows set in horsey villages. "Holy shit," I said when I saw it.

"Angela?" she said. "I'm Dr. Park. I was asked to come by."

I let her in. For convenience I've propped open the interior door.

"I understand you're on a hunger strike," she said. Her eyebrows were drawn toward each other, like she was worried, but they stayed there the whole time we talked. So either that's just how she looks or I'm someone who worries her.

She paused in the waiting room and held her bag with both hands. "Before we begin," she said, "you should know that my role is to confirm you are participating in this fast voluntarily, to evaluate your mental and physical health, including any underlying conditions that may make fasting more dangerous, and to provide you with medical care. I am not here to force-feed you. I am not here to spy on you, and I am also not here to serve as your spokesperson. For your safety, I may communicate basic information about your status to people outside this clinic, but I will not provide any further information or relay any messages without discussing the parameters with you in advance."

"That's serious," I said.

Eye contact. "I would say it's very serious."

"I'm into it," I said. "Let me show you my setup."

We headed back. I was planning to take her to room 4, which I don't go in much and which looks the most profesh, except for a spasming bulb. It occurs to me that this place—waiting-room chairs set up for slaloming, carpet unvacuumed, scent of old and new farts—is not at its best. It occurs to me I must have stopped slaloming chairs a couple days ago, and now I do not really, all that often, walk. This afternoon, leading the doctor, I was using the wall a lot, like we were part of each other. The hallway is getting longer.

"Let's go to the scale," she said. "There must be a scale?"

"Right," I said. I thought for a minute. In the nook by Dr. M's door. I see that scale a lot, but I've never succumbed. Exciting.

"OK, step on up," she said. "I'm sorry, but you can't hold on to anything." She slid the sliding things with a metallic flourish. "And what was your weight before you began fasting?"

"I don't know." (Lie.)

"Would you like an arm?" she said.

"What?"

Then I saw her arm, crooked and held out to me. Yes. We strolled together to this room, weird old room 2 with the double-table nest, because honestly I forgot to impress her with room 4. She picked up a piece of exam paper, this piece, halfway covered in writing. "Is there clean paper?"

Her fingers were warm, pressing at my pulse, my belly. She went to place the blood pressure cuff. "What's this?"

She meant the dent, still kind of oozy.

"A dent," I said. "On day 7 I dented myself."

"It's not healing," she said. She made a note.

She mixed up some water with lemon and salt and a vitamin concoction, made a little show of it. She found me some more pillows and explained to me, repeating certain phrases like a car alarm, some things *that could happen*. Hypothermia, sure, vision loss, the heart . . .

That WOULD happen, I tried thinking.

"I want you to understand"—she said suddenly, in the midst of her own speech—"that what I'm saying to you is just words. To actually go through it is something else."

Was she telling me how language works?

"I'll be back the day after tomorrow," she said. "Call me if you need me sooner." She left several cards.

"You're very professional" is I think what I said as she was leaving.

She looked curious?

"It's something I struggle with," I said. I tried: "Have a good night."

Realizing that when I said this it was 2 p.m.

Ever think of Rose who came with her own magazines tucked under her arm, like she didn't think she could waste time right with our supply? She was wearing a blouse and a flowy skirt with a careful crinkle. You could get abortions at the fancy hospital (like, Dr. Park's) but it costs way more so people come here. (Came here.) I think they found themselves surprised by the system in place, or their place in it. "Do you need anything else?" I asked Rose, who was just standing in front of my window, magazines tucked, holding the clipboard I'd given her, as if she wasn't sure where to go. It wasn't that there weren't seats. She turned to me and kind of smiled. "No, you've been great," she said (honestly?), "I was just expecting something different."

"Reality bites?" I said. That seemed neutral?

"The protestors don't seem that bad," she said. "I was really nervous about the protestors but they seem all right, it's just a few women."

"Well," I said, "you've never tried talking to them."

"Is it always like this?" she asked.

It was a sleepy midday, sun bright on the eyeballs and hot in the room, two kids were playing blocks on the floor in the corner while their mom typed fast on her phone, murmuring, I was wearing jeans with shredded knees and a tucked-in button-down with only one below-boob button missing, a compromise everyone could enjoy, the TV was on like hour 81 of some home renovation show where they were only touring houses built on the actual edges of actual cliffs, as if the minute filming ended a storm would just tip the whole thing into a big green sea. Between me and Rose were fingerprints on the glass and beyond her a carpet no one would call clean.

"Definitely," I said. "We're always just offering safe affordable reproductive healthcare for anyone who needs it." I'd heard Krys say this sentence, in a different tone.

"There's such a big price difference," Rose said, "between here and my ob-gyn through the hospital. I was really surprised. I mean, I was asking her, who would pay the higher price?"

"People who don't want to come here?" I said.

"But if you all are professionals," she said, then didn't finish.

I don't think I said anything. I was into anyone who would say that about me. What would happen next?

"Is it possible to get a little sip of water?" she said. "My throat is so dry. I guess I'm a bit nervous."

"We do have running water," I said. "But for you, no. Nothing by mouth."

From the doorway Monica called her name. Back she went.

Day 11

OK. More calls and mostly I don't answer. More little articles and so far they just state the basics: hey there's a hunger strike, here's Dr. M's case, she got 12 years. Adding nothing. This is helpful? The wording repeats from one bad site to another, garbage plagiarism. Who would pay to read this? Me, I guess. I'm in Donna's office, where I like to put in some time, curled up in her good wheely chair.

You're texting me about a . . . photo shoot? I think you're coming this afternoon. Can't totally follow. Sort of doesn't matter. I'm here.

Haven't seen you since—July? June? I remember there was air-conditioning. Longer gap than usual, but I don't like keep a diary. I mean, I guess this is a diary.

I guess I used to keep a journal, that's the word I used, in college. Started it right when I got there, ten years ago now, holy shit. "My journal."

There was a time you could say we were on-again off-again. Then a time that was more like, whenever we cross paths we fuck. Now I don't know, it's been a while.

Once you picked me up from work and Krys yelled, "Your friend's here!" No idea what she was talking about. When she pointed at you, I was like, what? You're not my friend.

I kept a journal in college, then I dropped out of college. That's when I met you and I never kept a journal again. Until now. So in the official record of my life this is your first appearance.

I don't mean I quit the journal because I met you. That like, the event of meeting you was so important. I was using the journal to think about something I had to stop thinking about.

When we first met I liked how you didn't ask questions. At that time in my life everyone was either asking me questions or not asking to spare me the embarrassment. Your not-asking felt different, like maybe you got it. I'm honestly not sure you know what I mean. It's like you wash the dish of each thought every time, right after you think it (I guess you don't wash actual dishes). I was at a house party like I thought I wouldn't go to again, since I'd gone off to college on this huge running scholarship, state champ gets recruited. But there I was. I was sitting in an overgrown yard that smelled green in the dark. Even in the dark I could see all these teeny daisies. I was sitting on the hood of a junked-out car, running my feet through daisies, they were tall and scratchy in a teeny way. I heard someone coming down from the house but I didn't turn. You stood for a sec by the driver's side door. I wasn't that drunk.

You said: "You look like you're just watching your own legs."

You were standing like any guy, beer in one hand, lit cigarette in the other. Too dark for faces.

"I am," I said.

"I can't tell," I said, "if they fucked me over or I fucked them over."

You took a drag. I thought you'd leave.

"You should just apologize either way," you said. "Even if it was their fault, just suck it up. They're nice legs and I don't think you're going to do better."

Did I nose-laugh? Sometimes I nose-laugh.

"Hand me your beer," I said.

I sprinkled beer on the ugly muscle above each kneecap. "You're welcome," I said to myself.

"I'm John," you said.

Before the journal, I was doing good. I was doing great. Anyone would say so. Everyone did. People had that well-look-at-you who'd-have-thought tone. After dicking around most of high school I'd won state, I'd gotten this unreal scholarship to a college people had even heard of, at least for sports. Everyone could stop worrying or judging or whatever they were doing. Finally all this had become a feel-good story, sit back and clap. Yeah, her mom died, and there were those DUIs, and she got kicked out of prom, and did have to take some pills for syphilis, probably not a secret, even the cops who got me the second time and whipped out the breathalyzer, they said hi to me by name the minute I rolled down the window trying not to piss myself. I'd fooled around with the trooper's little brother? Was that it? But all this got wiped clean or was just like the hero's backstory, OVERCOMING ADVERSITY, once I got that full ride and left the suburb we called a city, trophies tied to my bumper, not for real but basically. Well, I still couldn't drive till partway through freshman year, when I got my license back, but hey who was counting. The crowd stands and cheers.

And now here I was, spring of sophomore year, back already. Dropped out. Limping around, looking like shit, alone on the hood of some yard car, at a party thrown by assholes for assholes.

"I'm taking some time off school," I think I said to you, "to study the criminal justice system. Like, from the inside. Don't deal drugs." You nodded. Your silence is more of a fear thing than I realized. I just thought you were cool.

The journal fucked me up. No, it fucked me over. I was more scared of that journal than anything, which lasted honestly till now, when I came here, when I started this. When I chose to come here, start starving again, writing again. I'd started the journal when I went off to school. I am a *recruit*, I said to myself. I said to myself *college ball*, even though it was running. I wanted to feel serious. I couldn't keep feeling the opposite of serious. I'd never kept a training log. I'd never had a food log or a diet log or whatever you'd call it. I stayed thin like a shark stayed awake. But everyone at school was like *FRESHMAN 15!!!* and every Monday morning coach lined us up for the weigh-in. An assistant coach could have done it, captains could have done it, but he personally did it. For each girl he said the number out loud. Wrote it down in his book. He never had to look in his book for last week's number, he just knew, for every single girl. I started keeping my book because of his book. I thought it would prove I was on his level. Turned out my book worked for his.

Need a ride? you'd say whenever I needed a ride. You were never like, *what's with the arm hair? what happened to your teeth? what's your plan?*

It was like you were telling me you didn't need to know. Or that's what I thought.

We got into a rhythm. Cool. But then you thought you should be a boyfriend. I'm pretty sure you never wanted to be *my* boyfriend, so you got stuck either trying to be my boyfriend like you didn't want to but thought you were supposed to, or trying to break up with me, which wasn't even necessary. If you'd known me, you'd have known I didn't want to be known. Or like, dated. You got weird about the best thing about you. How not-curious you were. How you just let people be. That's when I had to start waiting for you to figure it out. Which brings us to now. The last few months I'm not sure which of us started mostly not-texting or not-texting-back. I'm gonna guess, using context clues, it was you.

You've had some girlfriends along the way, good for you. You'd be like, *I can't see you anymore, me and Claire are so serious . . . Danielle . . . Marissa . . .* Doesn't matter, I'd have said, not that you exactly asked, it's like buying beer for a drunk, it really doesn't matter what you do, same thing happens either way. You always turned back up. Until recently I guess you didn't. And I guess I don't leave well enough alone.

College was like: every Monday's weight, in the journal. Then every day's. Twice a day.

Every meal, calories added up, and the numbers gotta go down. Half an English muffin, dry. 3/4 cup of cornflakes, measured out, skim milk or water. Tofu cubed, cold and salted. Pinch of raisins. Carrot sticks with mustard. Pretzels with mustard. Mustard mustard mustard.

Numbers that had to go up: exercise, calories by hour (but always round down).

The fucking donut-looking mints, recorded, I learned to suck them so slow.

Every time I puked. Number of Tic Tacs.

My style was original. I was inventing both law and science. I was founding a new order. I was serious. My sweat smelled like fear, I got worried about that, my sweat and my breath. Traitors. Disgusting. It started to seem like the journal wasn't a record of events—what I was doing, though I thought of it like not-doing—but was the reason for those events. Like, if someone had said to me then, *you have a disease* (this happened later), I would have handed them the journal. I wouldn't have meant *here's the proof.* I'd have meant *here's the disease.* It seemed like if I hadn't started writing down what I was doing—not-eating, purging, they always say, why not just *puke*?—then I wouldn't have started doing it. The writing came after, but it was the cause.

Cardiomyopathy literally means *sick heart*?

"I'm afraid we're banning you from training, not just competition."

"Why are YOU afraid?" I probably said to whatever pointless faceless doctor this was. "This experience ends in like five minutes for you."

I pointed out that I'd been getting faster, which was the whole point of competitive running.

41 seconds off my fucking 5K, in less than a year, are you kidding.

But no, the rules had all changed.

"Some patients do have issues with fertility."

Even back then I'd had zero pregnancy scares.

I'd actually spent some time thinking about did I want to be a mom—like going back and forth, picturing it. When your mom dies you think about these things.

Waste of time, I guess. My journal decided.

You took the photos yourself.

It's night again and I guess I've been asleep. I guess you left around 6 and I slept for 3 hours.

I thought you'd have a photographer, like accompanying you, professionally. I thought you had a real job? You showed up all hoodie and stubble. I've only been here 11 days and it's not like I haven't seen people. At first people still looked normal. Then they didn't, or you didn't. It's like a 100° day in the Arctic (which my phone says just happened). How does some bird or plant up there even understand that. This is how people are to me now. Too much heat.

"Angela," you said, and I didn't move at all from the threshold. Behind you in the parking lot people were looking over, like they knew about me. "Can I come in?"

We were in the waiting room. With the windows boarded it's too fluorescent. Every way your face moved was too much.

When you leaned in to hug me I just stood there, even though, now that I can reflect, we always hug.

"Jesus, Angela," stubble awakening my face.

Stepping back you said: "The light's no good in here."

"We can go to the back."

If we'd ever been dating, or we'd ever been friends, there'd have been times we met up and didn't fuck. That's what relationships are. Every activity isn't foreplay. But what we liked about each other was fucking. Or fucking was the only door to whatever we liked. I didn't mind. I think I was happy. Don't think it's all clinical—some people with my problems fuck too much, I know, they get addicted, but I'm not like that. This was for you. Sleeping with other people was more to pass the time, test the waters, get out of a stupid moment.

Today we barely touched. Exam room 3. You stepped back, you arranged me and took photos. I felt like one of those bright red berries that glow in the weeds, and if an arm reaches out, a voice like my aunt's says: *no, that's poisonous.* Edible fruits are uglier, more skin, less light and more flesh. *Those are just for birds*, my aunt would say, as if there were animals who could survive on sickness. So many ways to survive, yet survival is just itself. You're either on the road or in the ditch.

"I don't know if I should be doing this," you said.

"I need more press," I said. "For this to work."

"Angela," you said, and you sounded very sure, "this is not going to work. Think about it. Does this country ever let anyone out of prison?"

I got to thinking about how my mom used to vote for Leonard Peltier for president. I think one time he ran and the rest of the time she just wrote him in. So I almost said, Leonard Peltier? But then I remembered, no. So far no one had ever let him out. He'd escaped once, I think, but even that hadn't worked. My mom knew a lot about this kind of thing. These were the things she needed to know. '70s, '80s, '90s, she kept everything fresh. *The phone would ring all through dinner*, she said. *Realtors, trying to get us to sell. Trying to scare us. All the white families were selling, they told us where they were moving to, the parks, the pools, what the houses were going for, how much less you'd get if you waited, boom boom boom, soon we were the last white family on the street. Don't let anyone tell you* (she used this phrase a lot, like stopping someone from telling you something was a power kids had) *white flight is just like a thing that happened. White people knew what they were doing. The phone rang all night.*

Yeah, her family moved too. Sometimes she got to that, mostly she left it out. Like we'd ended up in the suburb where we lived some other way. My aunt was the one to make a factual observation. *No one's stopping you from leaving,* she said to my mom, *if you don't like it.* Well, her kid might be stopping her, all those great suburban schools . . .

"Sorry," I said, because you'd been saying something. "What?"

"Let's do some like this," you said. You climbed up on an exam-room table and hugged your knees. The stirrups were in the shot. You were posed between them, hugging your knees. "Can you do that?"

You took a few. "Forget about the camera," you said. "Look at me like you're trying to convince me this will work. Look at me like I don't get it, but you can make me get it."

"Am I a big story for you?" I said at some point.

"I don't know," you said, but like you wanted to say yes. "I'm trying to drum up interest. Somewhere big. We'll see."

"Thanks," I said. I drank my lemony salty water.

"Don't thank me," you said. You reached out and encircled my tricep with your middle finger and thumb, which touched, easy.

I'd somehow forgotten you were you. I looked at your hand like it didn't belong to anyone.

"Could you do that before?" I asked.

You shrugged. "First time I tried."

Before leaving you stood in the waiting room scrolling through the photos in the back of the camera (you must have an actual job if you have an actual camera?). "Looking good," you said. "*You* don't look good, but the photos look good. I mean you look good under the circumstances."

"Remember when we first met? In the back of your car? Pullout in the backseat? I came here the next day, for the morning-after pill. That's how I first got reminded about this place. I saw there was a secretary-type job here and then my aunt helped me get it, or made me get it, I guess."

"I didn't know that," you said.

"How would you've known that?" I said. "That's not the point. Point is, this place makes people safe. It doesn't just make them *feel* safe."

You looked sad and smug. How do you pull that off? Did you say "You're not safe here anymore" or "It's not safe here anymore"? Either way you were right. But I'm not going to tell you that. I'm past that now.

When I think of my first visit here, I picture Krys handing me the white paper bag over the counter. It wasn't her, I don't think. Was it her? I tried to ask her once, but Krys always answers too hard. She treats every question like an invitation to a lifetime of future togetherness. Krys started here when her son was a baby, so that's what, ten, twelve years ago? She was just a kid, she says, and she needed the money. *I knew I had to work somewhere that mattered*, she'd say. Like people don't work wherever they have to. But Krys is stubborn. Reality pushes her around less than you'd think. She went back to school while she worked here, single mom living with her own mom. Every minute of her life must have been accounted for. Whenever her son comes by he's a real darling. He has manners. He says things like, *I don't want to make my mom late.* Once a few years back when he'd been dropped off and Krys was tied up, I tried to babysit. Or just like hang out. "Do you wanna come to the break room?" I said. "There's some candy." I didn't know this for sure, but someone would have something, a cookie I could borrow. "We can play a game." No plan for this either.

We walked down the short hallway. It's sweet when a kid puts their damp hand in your hand. Everyone smiled at the little dude. Janine, most people here are parents. "Are people going to jail?" he said.

"What?" I said. "Like in general?"

Would have been a great time to know anything, for example, about Krys, her family, her life, whatever. Maybe 2 out of 3 times she answers her phone in Spanish? It's like I'm always paying attention to the thing right next to the thing. It's annoying.

"Not here," I think I said. "We've got it all figured out here."

I said: "You'll be OK because you have a great mom." If I'm going to lie to kids I mix in some truth. I think they get that.

I think I got this job because in the interview I said one thing from college. I was in Donna's office, wearing a TJ Maxx suit jacket/skirt getup my aunt had shoved at me. I didn't wear stockings, though she'd told me to wear stockings, and in the fluorescent lights I could see my legs were a bony veiny mistake, my calf muscles looked like a freak golf ball problem. *I've been getting into the history of gynecology,* I said suddenly. *Like, the women who invented it. The actual history, which is their stories, which we'll never know.* Dr. M nodded, but said nothing. Why was Dr. M even there? She couldn't stand for decisions to be made without her. Otherwise the interview was just me repeating how fast I could learn to do things I had no idea how to do.

Before I worked here, I didn't get how much of medicine is hands. You change a body with your hand. Even pills started like that, though I'd never pictured it, plucking, boiling, crushing.

Like you invent something—the speculum, say, we've got lots of them—that throws open all these doors. See inside, glimpse the slick arrangement of organs. Which in this case have melted into and through each other. Fistula. Fistula means piss or shit leaks out the cunt. Infection, smell, mess, burning. A hell the baby leaves behind.

All day every day you'd sit on a stool with a hole cut in it. You'd trickle. You'd smell and you'd burn.

Usually the baby has died.

Dr. Sims—"father of modern gynecology"—had a little backyard hospital, if you could call it a hospital. His patients were all Black women who were slaves. They couldn't leave.

You get fistulas from bad nutrition. If he could keep the women alive and locked up long enough, cheap enough, he could invent a surgery he could sell.

Like if you already are so messed up you can't work, you can't have more babies for your owner to sell, then maybe your owner gives consent. For some experiments, which the doctor says will be a treatment. After a couple years the doctor gets less popular. It's taking too long, the women are screaming too loud, and his assistants all quit. The women, enslaved, become his assistants, he says. They want the surgery, he says. For the operations they hold each other still. According to him. The women don't leave any records. 3 names—Anarcha, Betsey, Lucy—though there were more than 3. No anesthesia. It took years. Over 4 years Anarcha had 30 surgeries, his records say. No anesthesia—that's the main thing I remember.

Picture, like, the think-therefore-I-am guy nailing a spring through the paw of a dog. I learned about it. Because animals have no souls (he said), their screams were just mechanical (he said) reactions.

Sims killed babies, for real. Over and over he tried to fix tetanus (he said). He believed the skulls of Black people grew too fast. He took an awl to the skulls of new babies. Tetanus kills but he killed faster.

Then one day he stitched shut a fistula. For the first time the stitch held. Silver thread. The body healed. Anarcha healed. His records don't say if he ever cured Lucy or Betsey once he learned how. He didn't bother to record it or didn't bother to do it?

No way to picture all that. You can't. When I try, I picture the women as us—all of us here—which is all wrong. When I picture it, I never picture Dr. M as the doctor. I picture her with the women, as a woman, one of us. That's not what she'd choose, I think, for someone to imagine. But guess what, she doesn't get to choose.

Day 12

You need me to say it?

I wasn't dealing. Never have. I don't touch pills.

Drunk driving, of course. That's my record, that's all there is, just like a lot of it. The last one was a big one, DUI-extra-plus, and everything that ever happened before counted against me. Sometimes it's not about how much you drink but how little of you there is. If you weigh 92 pounds it's not hard to spike the old BAC. 30 days in jail, 2 years probation. And I wasn't even 21. Huge-ass fine and my aunt had to help me out. Lost my license again—and I'd just gotten it back after all the high school shit—this time for a year. As long as we're being real, since then I don't drive. I can now but I don't. I take the bus. I walk. I do not like bikes. You've seen me walking. I think like one out of three times we hooked up it was just because you saw me, somewhere in the city, walking. Or we'd both be somewhere—some party, or that one time, a couple years back, at a fundraiser thing for my aunt—and you'd give me a ride home. You just assumed. "I'll take you home," you said, not a question. Those were probably my favorite times.

Anyone could kill someone. If you want to kill someone without admitting that's what you're jonesing to do—well, drunk driving is how. Me, that last time, I thought I'd killed someone. I couldn't figure it out. I could have. There's nothing I could have, in the moment, changed. I hit a tree but if it had been another car, like with three kids lined up in the backseat. Boom. I'd have hit them. Simple. When I was sitting next to my car, fucked-up by airbags, windshield smashed up and hood crumpled, big flesh wound in the tree, a cracking open that smelled fresh and woody, I kept picturing three kids, in a backseat. I kept thinking—it didn't line up—*you killed her.* I tried to throw up but I couldn't. Ironic? I could have run. I could have left the car where it was and run. Then they couldn't have tested me, I get that now. They couldn't have got their cop hands on my drunk blood. The evidence. Without that it was just an accident, dummy hits a tree. Sad girl dummy, just lost her shot at the Olympics. Not even. Her shot at what, like one season All-American? I sat there, not-puking. *You killed her.* Those kids those kids, I thought, even though I knew it was just a tree. I could smell it, I could hear the leaves of the cracked branch sweep against the busted glass. The woods were forever. I was pretty far off the road. You're all alone, I thought. I didn't run.

I was remembering—I remember remembering—a girl I knew. She was dead. We weren't friends when she died. She was 15—we were both 15, but she stopped there. In sixth grade we'd been friends but then she'd gone to a different junior high. Anyway we probably wouldn't have stayed friends. She was good at school, she got called out of normal class to go to the special invisible classes. In sixth grade we were in some normal science class with a bitch teacher. One of those teachers who, when you look back, seems like pure evil, like she took that job just because then she could make kids cry. I don't think she cared a lot about, what, volcanoes or whatever she was supposed to be teaching. Rocks making younger rocks. Marie and I would sit together in the back. I don't think Marie had ever hated someone like she hated that teacher and it was like, in that rage, I was her coach. No, not even, we were together in this mission. She was willing to give up on being a good student just to prove this was the worst possible teacher. What was our resistance even? Passing notes. Talking back. Encouraging anyone who talked back. Once when Mrs. Miller had screamed so hard and so long she'd made a girl cry again— when she, an adult getting paid, watched in silence as this girl, a little kid, was sobbing in public almost too hard to pick up the bathroom pass (the only escape possible) from the blackboard tray, Marie stood up and followed the girl straight out of the room, no pass, breaking the rules, just to go comfort someone, just to be on their side, just to say with her back as she walked out the door, *fuck you*. I was proud. As Marie walked out Mrs. Miller was screaming her name but she didn't turn. That's right.

But then all that was over, we got older, off to different schools, different fates. And one day in tenth grade in study hall I was listening in on some convo. I didn't have a goal, I just liked eavesdropping, I would put my head down on the desk and hear everything around me. People thought I was on something but I wasn't, I was just creepy. Two girls were talking about a girl who'd died that weekend, from the next school over. Someone's cousin's friend. Then they said her full name. I looked up.

My mom always got the local paper and when I got home I looked through it, I checked every day and searched online till the obit appeared. *Remember her?* I asked my mom. *Remember, I went to her birthday party, in like 6th grade? Marie,* my mom said, *she had nice eyes and a drinky mom.* My mom read the obit and then said (everything was a fucking lesson): *her boyfriend was 19. That's a bad age gap, 15 to 19. Promise me you won't date a 19-year-old, not till you're that age.*

Why is everything a fucking lesson? I probably said. *The point is just that she's dead. For no reason. She's dead.*

People said that the guy—her boyfriend—had been driving and crashed. He'd gone off the road hard, and somehow she'd flown—through the glass?—out of the car. Unbuckled? She died. Her body was on the ground, found there, alone. Beneath a tree her body had hit. There was no car. He'd driven away. Because he was drunk, you had to figure. But they'd never prove that part. They couldn't prove it because he ran. He drove off, he took the fucked-up car and he left. She died there alone. People said it took hours, however they know things like that. She was 15 and all alone when she died.

So I guess that's why, that night, five years or whatever later, I didn't run. I got everything confused and I sat there waiting. *You killed her.* Things never got clearer. I'd already run from something once that night so in my mind I was done. Running a second time would be like waking up from a dream into a worse dream. No way back. I think I thought something like that. I'd gotten in the car to run from the party. It was an actual frat party at my actual college. After break, after I got my license back the first time, I'd brought my mom's piece-of-shit car back with me to school, and now that was done. I hadn't planned to drive home that night. I'd thought things through. I'd drive to the frat, good outfit, good shoes, then at the end of the night I'd grab sneakers from the trunk, walk the hour home. Run out there the next day and pick up my car. Not rocket science. And the long walk helps block the hangover. But things went sideways. Or they went normal and I had to get what normal was. It's a frat party, what did you expect? *You killed her.* But I'd seen—we'll say L, let's call her L—I'd seen her, like exactly how you'd picture, draped on a bed in a room. 3 guys in there. Hockey. *Hockey,* I'd said earlier that exact night, *is the fucking worst.* L and I, teammates, freshman year we always hit the same times, it was eerie. I'd fucking die to clip her at the end of a workout but we'd come in together, stride for stride. Sophomore year, when I lost the last 8 pounds, down to 92, then I could drop her. *You killed her.* L was a little bulky, real strong.

Coach kept giving her shit about it, why couldn't she lose 10 pounds, look at me, dropping her. Leaving her in the dust. That night in the frat house I could see her strong thighs, through the half-open door to the room, like a movie. The skirt ridden up or flipped up. What did you expect? What are you, surprised? I was going to scream, outside the door, but I just ran. I didn't have one single thought, I just got downstairs, using the railing, using the wall, found the door of the house, found the door of my car. I put my hands on the wheel. My arms were nothing. I could see them, for once, clearly. They were little twigs a cartoon bluebird could break. The house had been kind of empty. Almost empty. I didn't want to scream because I didn't want the 3 of them to turn and see me, grab me, drag me in. I was too drunk to actually stand, to actually run. 93 pounds, counting the vodka. 3 of them, hockey. At least she was passed out, I thought. Is that a thought? If I'd screamed there could have been help, I could've helped, the house wasn't totally empty. I want to be clear that driving like that is like nothing people do in the actual world. It's a little death tour, a preview. I don't remember seeing but the feeling of seeing. I couldn't tell what anything was. Everything was kind of working, I was on the road, then I wasn't. Everywhere glass was broken, breaking through the whole fucked world. Later I learned a sliver just missed my eye. I listened to the tree branch, sweeping against the face of the night. *You killed her.*

And L? I never saw her at practice again because I never went to practice again. I got arrested, I was banned. At first I was just arrested, but then once everyone was looking at me, once the athletic director met with me and looked at me, I got shipped off to bitch doctors who announced I had a sick heart. And that was that, no more team, the end. Back then I thought the problem was street clothes, that they'd seen me in street clothes, because that's when you look skinny. As long as you're in running clothes, it all kind of works, they don't notice how they can see like the freaky ball of your hip joint or the exact line where your tricep hits bone. But on reflection it wasn't the street clothes, it was the heart scan that finished me, also the scale.

Honestly L was the only one on the team who'd made sure to loop me in, to invite me to things, to check in. She had this low-key way to her. Like whatever nice thing she said was no big deal. Women in my family are really not like that. I don't know what happened to her that night. I don't know what happened to her any night since. When I could have helped her, I didn't. When I could have helped myself, I didn't.

I ran, I didn't run. That's it.

I always thought one day someone would ask me one follow-up question. About dealing, I mean, this story I always told like it was better than the truth. Name one pill, one price. And just like that, my cover would be blown. Dealing seemed like a better story because it was, like, active. You were just a temporarily failed businessman. But actually I don't have some cool story. More like I used to be a cool story but I fucked it up, the one thing I was good at, forever. But anyway no one asks. Maybe everyone already knows. They're, like, sorry for me. To my face they don't say it. Maybe everyone just thinks I'm a liar. So nothing I say even matters.

"I'll take you home," you'd say.

"Need a ride?" you'd say.

You knew I didn't drive, but you never asked. Back then I thought this was nice. Now I think maybe you didn't want to get into it. What would happen if we got into it?

You knew I liked fucking you. What if I told you what I liked about it? Not just what I wanted one night or another. What was particular to you. Between us something like that—if I'd said something like, how you moved my hair off my face so you could see my expression—that would have been treated like a big declaration. No one could say the first thing. If you'd said to me—I know it's true—that what you liked was to get up after, fill my water bottle at the sink and bring it back to me in bed, make fun of how you'd never seen me without it. Standing behind me at the bathroom mirror, running the back of one finger slowly down my high spine. Fucking was the path to this place. Turned up high the fan was a wild wind. You'd hand me the controller so that in the game—very late, naked—I could drive hard off the highway into a desert twilight, in the pixel shadow of stucco condos, get out and run, hop on some video-game Ferris wheel and dive off at the peak of its turn into a video-game sea. You were laughing. I remember you laughing.

Dr. Park returned. Noon, on the button. She looked at me and said, "I'm going to come every day from now on."

"That was fast," I said.

"Is this a good time for you? It's my lunch break."

She set me up on a table, stethoscoped a little.

"I see you've had other visitors."

"What?" I looked around.

"There's photos," she said, "online."

"Good," I said. "I mean, are they good?" I reached for my phone.

"Artsy," she said.

"These will help," I said, scrolling. I figured out what you were up to. Put a couple up on Instagram, shop the rest. Were you shopping the rest?

"If you want my opinion," Dr. Park said, "they're a little glamorous. Like you're a model and this was some kind of fashion shoot."

"What should I look like?"

"In my experience," she said, "a protest like this works best when people know exactly what they want and who can make that happen."

"OK," I said. "Sounds like you've seen some highly effective people starve themselves to death."

I think Dr. Park's patience is in a love-hate relationship with her lack of patience. She paused then said: "If a hunger strike goes well, no one dies. But if you're asking if I'm here with you because of my professional experience, the answer is yes. It was some time ago, but I helped treat undocumented workers, refugees in Europe, who went on hunger strike to try to gain legal status, work and residence permits. The strike was in Brussels, and I went there from Berlin, where I was doing research at the time. It was intense, medically, since a number of workers participated, in a few waves."

"Did they get what they wanted?"

"Some did and some didn't. Some of the gains were temporary."

"But it didn't change things like for everyone. For every refugee in the future."

"No."

"And no one died?"

"Not while I was there. But people got very sick. One man from Morocco fell from a construction crane, which a group of workers on hunger strike had been occupying. Others had failing kidneys, intestinal blockage, serious problems."

"Still an OK record, for you."

"My role only lasts a few weeks. It's a question of people's whole lives."

She did the blood pressure thing.

"You were underweight when you began fasting," she said. "So the dangerous part may start a little sooner for you. You may have less time than people you've read about. If you did research to prepare."

"Not really," I said, "or not like you're thinking."

She asked: "Have you heard from Fatima?"

"Dr. M?"

"Yes."

"No."

I was lying flat on my back on the table. Dr. Park lay the back of her hand briefly on my forehead, as if to check my temp, which she'd already, with a thermometer, officially read.

"I exchanged messages with her," she said, "through the prison email system. I suggested she communicate with you through her attorney or her son."

"Dr. M is usually pretty direct with me, so."

"She doesn't seem hopeful right now. I would say she's lost hope. But I knew her best when we were young—about your age—on a fellowship together, a long time ago now. So I don't know her well anymore. And not everyone needs hope. It doesn't seem like you do."

She smoothed my hair off my forehead, twice.

"I guess not," I said.

"She said to thank you, but she said it's not necessary. Meaning your protest. I thought you should know she said that. Those were her words. *It's not necessary.*"

"OK," I said. "Thanks."

I said: "And what was Dr. M like when she was my age?"

"She was very focused." Dr. Park paused and I heard a sound like a roach getting bold in the light. "She was volunteering a lot, traveling to places where sexual assault was used as a weapon in war. When I met her she was just back from the former Yugoslavia. She used to say she was following the path of the crime. And it was always ahead of you or beyond you. For any assault, you could help with the effects of it, you could train people and help set up clinics, postpartum care, contraception access, all that, but you could never come to terms with what had happened. She used to say she had been summoned there by the criminal."

"Sounds heroic," I said. Very Dr. M.

"Yes," Dr. Park said slowly, "but it was something else too. She was always saying that we shouldn't shy away from their language—the other side's language, the violence of it. If they say abortion is murder, you can agree. *There isn't another language*, is how she'd put it, *healing and harm aren't so different*. To be honest I never quite saw her point. In medicine it's important how we talk about what we do and it's not so hard to frame things for your audience."

"But you probably heard her talk like this yourself," Dr. Park said.

"Dr. M didn't really share her whole philosophy with me," I said.

Something was bothering me: "If you two met on a big fancy fellowship," I said, "how come you're working at the big fancy hospital and she's at the neighborhood corner abortion store?"

"This clinic does very important work."

"But we're not like some war-torn do-gooder scene. Like Angelina Jolie isn't going to visit this strip mall."

"Maybe that's exactly the reason," Dr. Park said.

Did Dr. Park feel bad she hadn't kept up with her do-gooding? Is that why she was here, sacrificing her lunches?

"I actually didn't know Fatima worked here," she added. "I had no idea until her arrest. I hadn't seen her in years."

"Rest up," she said, and rose. She pointed toward the water bottle. "Hydrate. And give some thought," she added, "to what we talked about."

Visible in her unzipped purse on the counter was a beautiful lunch, beautifully packed, in glass containers with tops that perfectly sealed. She slipped the purse over her shoulder and walked, not turning back, out the door.

Day 13

Alive alive.

I woke up saying this to myself.

Woke up a few times and said this.

Hungry.

Alive.

Brought a bucket in here (room 2) as bathroom alternative. But then I have to drag it to the bathroom. Put a clipboard across the top to block the smell. Thought about writing TOILET on a piece of paper, clipping it in place, in case anyone else wants to use it, I guess.

Now that we're shut down I can use the patient bathroom, which is closer, but I've been walking to the staff bathroom, which is smaller and farther away. In the patient bathroom I don't like picturing everyone pissing on their own hands, holding a sample cup in the hot stream. And it's too big, you can't lean on the wall.

Everything smells like shit but I am very very very very very very hungry. I thought smell was like 9/10 of eating, or the law, or whatever.

Just thought of like a jar of honey mustard, with those big old seeds in it, like I'd eat it straight off a knife, who cares if I'd puke it back up. Might be a packet of regular yellow left in the break room, don't think about it.

Very very very very should write about something else

Reporter who called me last night was so slick. Like are there salons where you can get your voice waxed. Content-wise he was just kind of thinking aloud. "I've never been out there," he said, meaning this city. I thought reporters would feel more pressure to be interesting.

"Flyover country," he said.

"Original," I said.

He sort of laughed.

Question like: "It seems to me like you're trying to create a sense of urgency around protecting reproductive rights, as well as protesting the criminalization of abortion providers like your former boss. Is that how you'd put it?"

"Sure," I said.

For the rest of the convo (I was on Dr. M's baby couch, where I conduct business) I kept my eyes closed. Roaches were getting all the way in, under my eyelids. I had to think hard to keep my teeth from chattering. So I couldn't think about anything else. I tried to come up with something someone would say. I pictured Monica, with her clipboard, how she watched situations get going. Like when I was a kid playing double Dutch, waiting to hop in, eye on the circling ropes. She'd observe, plan her move, perfect entrance. OK.

"She's not a criminal," I said.

"But since she was convicted and sentenced under the new state law, it's unlikely she'll be released in response to your protest. How concerned are you about the likelihood you'll succeed? Do you see your protest as more symbolic?"

"No," I said. "I mean, I'm actually starving. I promise you it's really happening. So, I'm asking for her to be released, but that also isn't the point. The point is she shouldn't be in there. The point is people should care that she was put in prison just for helping people."

"I agree, people should care, and you're taking a big risk to try to get their attention. But since she was convicted of what is now a crime in your state, I'm just wondering about your goals, from a practical standpoint—"

"Do you ever think about, like, the other guys crucified all around Jesus? Like, just normal so-called criminals who happened to be there?"

Was he writing, in his little notepad, *thinks her boss is Jesus*? Fuck. But I'm pretty sure I kept going. I could hear what was happening but I was in the flow. I was trying to tell him like:

"They were just regular criminals. They were convicted, which is how they got up there, on their own personal crosses, with all the blood going to their feet, and their bones dislocating just from gravity. Eventually did you know your chest is so stretched out you can't breathe, and to breathe you have to use your legs, push yourself up, even though your feet are nailed down, you have to push yourself up for the length of the breath. Did you know that random people would come by and break your legs with a club, to be nice, so you'd die faster?"

He didn't know that.

"That's what I'm talking about," I said. "Mike, what I mean is, it doesn't matter, in that moment, what they did, like what their crime was, if they did anything."

"My name is Steve," he said.

Unbelievable. That really got me.

What I meant was: "You live in your body, but at all the important moments, it's beyond you. You just have to wait. You have to pray for mercy, you have to hope someone will come and break your legs. The law says, this is a crime, this is not a crime. Whatever. That's all on the surface level. The body lives on a level beyond that. Like, just because boats know about icebergs and whales know about icebergs doesn't mean boats can talk to whales. You know? You don't get it. The law is over here, it's up here, it's on the surface. When someone gets pregnant, it has to do with her up-here life, but it's really a conversation the body is having with other bodies, including itself. You can hear it when it gets loud. When it shuts off your period, you get fat, you get pukey. In moments like that you have to listen. You have to cross over, you have to put your head underwater and listen. You have to find someone who understands how things work in this other place. This is why we all feel like totally helpless when we see doctors, and we think they're so amazing or evil. Because most of our life happens somewhere we can barely get to and don't understand."

What I meant was: "It's just saying *living living living dying dying dying.* Doctors don't want to hear this either, but they do. That's why they're always saying bullshit like *she's going to be*

OK, which they definitely do not know. But sometimes we can just listen, we can just hear it and it's OK. In my opinion this is how sex works. Sex opens the door. You go right into the place you're always avoiding, there you are. Your body knows you're there and it's like, OK, follow me, I know the rest of the way. And it's so hard if you have to find your way back on your own, just you by yourself. You need help just to try. Someone has to help you all the way back to halfway to that place. They can help you. It's like, if you're dying on the cross, they come and break your legs. They listen only to the body and they speak to it in its own fucked whale-song language. The body always knows about dying. You're the one who doesn't know. I don't mean you in particular, Steve, or whatever, I mean anyone. What I mean is, Dr. M has a hard job, and everyone just lies about it. They know they don't want to know. They're scared of how much they are like every single other body, every single one is completely out of control and could die or not die at any time. But when you need it she'll come over here and break your legs. Or do whatever. And we're all part of it, or we were before you closed us down. That's what I'm saying. The law can't get at what this is about."

Whatever I actually said he couldn't deal. He didn't get it. More questions. I said:

"Steve, someday you're going to do the best job of your life and then a bunch of professionals are going to ask you a bunch of dumbass questions, and in that moment I will be your best friend. Forget anything I said. The hunger strike is talking. I'm saying what it's saying. She was just doing her job, and her job is helping people, and they should let her out. I'm willing to do this to say that. People who think abortion should be rare or just in a few cases, people who think that in a perfect world no one would need an abortion just can't handle reality. Abortion is so real. Have you ever noticed that when people talk about it they say the realest things? This is real. The hunger strike. I personally probably can't even get pregnant and I'm willing to do this."

Something something about fertility or my "lived experience"?

"Omg Steve, who cares. *Anorexic slut starves herself to death for boss who would rather have fired her.* Blah blah blah. Listen to what the strike is saying. It's cool and unique. I shouldn't have to say anything else. It's a great story, you just have to write it. You can do it."

Day 14

You can do it?

Pretty sure that's what I said.

Well I've got lots of time to regret it.

You can do it? That's what that old guy used to say to me. From the bench by the bus stop on that slow run I used to try to do. He was always there. Don't know what rare bus he was waiting for. A few years ago I thought I might run again. At that point it had been a clean 4 years since I got banned, seemed like I'd served my time, 4 years like a college degree, not that I had one. I laced up the old sneaks. The loop I liked took me out around the big destination cemetery and through a neighborhood to the east, up the tall slope of the overgrown park, out by the car dealership, hang a right home. I started out running then walking, running then walking. Running wasn't too different from walking. My shins hurt and the ball of each hip. My shoulders hurt from holding my arms up and my neck hurt from the weight of my head. My heartbeat was not right exactly, it had its own style. And every 10 feet spit totally coated my molars. I hocked. I couldn't tell what I wanted. To be fast again? Drop 10 pounds? Win something no one cared about? I was seeing the city. Living in it and through it. Running is a sweet way to pass through it. But it's not personal. If you were walking you'd be a person. You could feel out of place. When you're running you're just a runner. You're passing through. No one, you included, wonders who you are, why you're there, it's self-evident. Anything awkward is brief. You're moving faster than anybody you brush by. Sure one time I ran right down a hushed street where everyone else was dealing drugs—two huge silver Lexuses pulled up to a half-decayed house—and I didn't take that street again. But I was where the city was. Most people—try anyone—don't know the whole of the city. People have their routes, a series of lines they groove into, work to home to grocery store, whatever. Stare out the window of the bus, pass the proud one-star daycare. Just here to there. If you're poor and you work in a rich neighborhood, you go there. If you're rich when do you go somewhere poor? Is it always a choice, an activity you're performing with the right footwear and your insured teeth? When you're running your presence justifies itself. It's not that you're welcome everywhere, you're not. But you're self-contained, a person whose intentions are transparent and stupid. No worries, just this.

You can do it! I heard at an intersection where I paused to hit the button, wait on the light. Shuffling my legs in place, listening to the freaky thump-thump. I looked over and an old guy was smiling. He lifted his cane springily and shook it,

You can do it! then went back to whatever he'd been thinking about. I was offended for sure. I was the champion of the entire state, every single high school. I knew I could do it. Who thought I couldn't? It was like I was about to ask, *Do you know who I am?* I had to shake my head at myself, plodding on up the park's forever hill. That hill got me. I walked, I leaned over and planted my hands on my thighs, like a training montage in a waiting-to-be-heartwarming sports movie. I realized I'd graduated. Not from college, but from something else. Instead of catcalls you get, like, sympathy. You're not the usual everyday loser, you're a real loser, worth shouting at, they could make after-school specials about you. People are into that. The guy at the bus stop got it. He'd lost a few rounds himself. Like hey, did you forget there's a new state champ every year, no one cares. So this was—I realized as I reached the summit of the hill, picked some dead grass out of the top of my sock—the nicest thing anyone had ever said to me. *You can do it.*

Saw him on that loop often. He cheered, every time.

Then my shin cracked in half—stress fracture, bullshit bones—and I was done running. Again.

From the summit of the hill in the park you could see all the way to the dirty big lake, flat bluer smudge below the low blue of the sky. I had a plan to run out that way, like I used to, run to the breakwater where you could find dudes fishing mildly, a barbeque, couples who'd stepped out onto the platform beyond the high rocks to make out where only the lake could see them. Gray cats sliding out from between gray rocks, lake cats looking for left-out bait. Sometimes you'd spot a thoughtful circle of cat food slapped on a warm rock. Seagulls dove and cried out. I couldn't see any of this from the hill, but I could, I knew everything was there, and beyond it the lighthouse, red and white like a candy cane above the bright water. Between me and the horizon was the long hill, in winter kids sled down it way too fast. According to high school teachers and signs on endless vacant buildings, we used to be a big town for shipping, for iron, for steel, for sewing machines, for oil, for paint, for cars, for answering services, for restaurant menus, for the atom bomb.

Now, not much. Even the abortion industry, shutting down.

The river that feeds the lake is best known for how many times it's caught fire.

Someone told me that gasoline was discovered here, all the oil refineries kept shitting their waste into the river, it kept catching fire, again and again, then they realized, lightbulb, what a gold mine.

I don't think you can trust one thing this city says about itself. Even if it claims to be the start of the end of the world.

From the summit I made my way back into the park, avoiding shiny stacks of deer stool littered on the hillside. The last couple times I tried to run my shin hurt so bad I'd run out a few miles, then hobble my way back, very slow, it took hours. Long grass swept against my legs and I pictured little poison ticks crawling up up up. I passed a small waterfall with its rockface graffiti, I was limping, so slow and hard, and a

teen who was sitting there writing fast in a notebook turned
at the sound of me, then turned away without saying a word.

Do you think L still runs? I could look her up on the socials.
I've tried. She has a common name, first last combo. I deleted
everything when I left school so I'd have to find everyone all
over again. I wouldn't want L to see me on there, lurking and
looking. I think people know how to see you. It's not like she
knows I saw her that night through the door. I don't think she
saw me see her. But it all works out the same. I left, I got
arrested, back on my bullshit, and if she needed anything, like
a ride to a place like this after a night like that, I wasn't there.
In the end she only ran OK in college, I heard she got a pelvic
fracture junior year that took her out. I like to picture her now
living in a cute town and dominating the local 5K, one of those
hard moms who can annihilate all the joggers while gliding a
stroller uphill. I'm thinking, it could kind of suck for her if she
heard from me now.

Once when I got to work late I heard everyone talking about
that same park. Whenever I was late, which was always, I'd
walk in on some conversation being waved in front of me,
some morsel for early birds. Part-time Stevie was quoting a
podcast on the subject of the city we all lived in. Apparently
this podcast was discussing the criminal justice system of our

city as an example of the injustice of the American criminal justice system. They claimed it wasn't personal, we were chosen for exactly how typical we were, but come on.

Why do you need a podcast to tell you about the place you've lived your whole life, I started to say to Stevie, but then someone said the name of that same park up whose hill I'd lately been, like a low-budget girl Rocky, sucking wind. Talked about in the podcast, and which I guess would have been—but let's be honest, probably was not—in the news was some extreme police violence that happened there. The park was where the cops drove guys they wanted to rough up before they took them in. For this guy it went especially bad because he tried to escape. He ran into the woods. But they caught him. In the dark, if you didn't know where the trail was, you'd be fucked.

"Good place to choose," I said.

Everyone looked at me. Stevie tidied a folder. "What now, Angela?"

"I just mean," I said, "no one's ever in that park. If you want to do something without getting seen doing it, it's a good place. I run there all the time and no one's ever around."

"You shouldn't run there, then," someone said. "That's not safe."

I got stuck on that because I always feel like, if you admit you think something isn't safe, you've given someone somewhere a weapon whose use you can't control. Later I listened to the podcast myself and learned the cops had kicked the man all the way down that huge hill. He's had bad headaches since.

He can't work. When he complained and the city eventually surprisingly punished the cops, things got worse, not better, for him, since from then on cop after cop has sought him out to mess with in retribution. Because you got beat you have to get beat. What if a deer had been there that night, an antsy young buck with big fuzzy antlers? Could he have run full speed into this human scene? But cops famously have guns. What would I have done? If I'd been running by right then? Cops don't beat up young white women too often, with the exception of their own personal girlfriends. But wouldn't they arrest you for being there, they'd come up with something? And my probation had just ended. But maybe just by saying something, I could have . . . By appearing, like a reminder of something . . . none of this happened.

Still, at the bottom of the hill I'd picture the man sometimes, I imagined extending a hand, leading him along the overgrown trails to escape. Watch my feet and you won't trip.

But no one was there to help him. No one helped him at all.

Come to think of it, no one's here to help me.
Unlike every single patient who ever
Rose after Rose after Rose
I am here by myself. I am alone here.
Head pounding, stink, don't want to lift my head.
Is my pulse right?
Blood like exploding, bam bam bam. Cheeks, teeth, small and hard.

Would love some room-temp blue Gatorade and those pink little licorice pellets.

Dr. Park comes then goes.

I swear the roaches are multiplying.

It's not necessary

Was that what I was supposed to think about? Or the other thing Dr. M said, forever ago?

Summoned there by the criminal

Yes I was.

Monica & part-time Stevie & even Donna were always trying to get Dr. M to up our security. Stevie would dog-ear a magazine her boyfriend got in the mail like a perv. Upgrades to window glass, locks, panic buttons, camera systems. We got mailings with coupons. Dr. M shook her head.

"She doesn't remember," Monica would say. She'd wait till Dr. M had headed toward the back but Dr. M could still hear. "She wasn't living in the States when guys were bombing clinics, walking into clinics and just shooting people. Snipers waiting for doctors. One guy was holding, like, a bowl of soup for his son, turning to put it on the table, and he was shot through his kitchen window right then."

"One guy"—Monica looked at me—"shot two receptionists in one day. Two clinics. He walked into the first, shot the receptionist in the throat with a rifle, left, walked to the next nearest clinic, shot the receptionist there."

So I said: "After one clinic was bombed, they hung a big sign on the construction site that was rebuilding it. HELL NO, WE WON'T GO. Then they opened right back up."
While they were talking I'd read this on Wikipedia.
They treated me like I wasn't one of them, but I got it.
"Who cares whether I lived here then?" Dr. M would say.
"You hardly need to live in America to know American violence."

Rose didn't always say anything, or not to me, but sometimes I thought I could tell. She'd carry herself like her entire self had betrayed her. After a second-trimester job, Dr. M washed her hands a while then walked up and sipped from a reusable straw out of a reusable cup she kept on the far end of my desk like I didn't work there. She started talking to me like I'd asked her a question, like I did anything besides shoveling people and forms back and forth in bad light. A dictator, she was saying, who'd passed a bunch of laws. After that, thousands of victims of rape were jailed, sometimes flogged, sometimes sentenced to death by stoning (though usually aren't you lucky they didn't end up carrying that out). Laws stayed on the books for decades. If you accused someone of rape and you couldn't prove it, you'd get charged with adultery, fornication. To prove anything you had to have 4 adult Muslim men on your side, like swear-to-God witnesses. Women's testimony was nothing. It counted for nothing. So girls and women got locked up for years for the crime of their own rape.

I used to have a chair that made a fun squeak when you rocked back and forth, till Donna fixed it.

Dr. M said: "If I tell most Americans" (she whipped her hand around at the clinic and sounded a little bit vicious) "about all that, they'll think it's another story about backward Muslims in a backward country. But the dictator was backed by the US. America loved him, they kept him in power over us, used him to fight the Cold War and destroy hundreds of villages. This is an American story."

She didn't say if she thought I was different, I'd get it, though that's what she was implying (was it?) by telling me. Or she didn't care what I thought, so I was a perfect audience, like talking to a drunk pane of glass.

But didn't I get it?

"Well here we have this great system where if you're raped you won't go to jail, but then neither will he."

Did I say that?

Here I am, all by myself on Dr. M's couch, mouth rotting like an old rape kit.

Maybe Dr. M didn't tell us what she was up to because we never ever shut up. Maybe it was, like, calming to do a bunch of abortions without hearing us all sharpen our knives on each other. I get it, Dr. M. Sometimes you gotta go it alone.

And for years we'd been crying or smart-ass-ing our way through all the hallway-size laws all the janitor's-closet-size laws all the clinic-must-be-at-least-2000-feet-from-a-public-school laws all the temperature-in-clinic-must-be-between-75-and-80-degrees-Fahrenheit-and-between-50-and-60-percent-humidity laws all the garbage-cans-must-be-kept-entirely-clean laws all the hospital-admission-privilege laws all the patient-transfer-agreements-with-hospitals-are-required-for-abortion-clinics-to-have-but-patient-transfer-agreements-with-abortion-clinics-are-illegal-for-hospitals-to-make laws all sent to little government men by an army of think-tank Janines, signed sealed delivered. Around us clinics kept closing. And this was before they dropped the big one. Eventually there'll be just like one abortion clinic left in New York, one in LA. They'll each smell exactly like Gwyneth Paltrow. And I think everyone knew the whole time this was where things were going. We didn't know how they'd get us there but I think we knew, someday it'd just be us and the phone screaming and no help coming. If you're in a state like this, goodbye healthcare, hello more fentanyl. Which is something, I guess, I mean it'll take the edge off.

I need Steve's/Mike's article to come out. I don't feel clear. I need some takes, some comment threads. I don't know why I thought writing a journal would help, unless someone reads it and tells me what it all means.

And why is Steve the new John? 14 days in, like my hunger strike is ovulating, I could have a new little baby hunger strike, and John has done nothing. You took some photos. OK. The whole time we were not-dating I was like *this guy has a job*. I liked that about you. It was something distinguished, what a professional, he went to a good school. But maybe you're a reporter like we were dating? So, not? I never read your articles, or like once a year I'd scroll around. They seemed fine, I mean, I didn't know all that stuff about city council and the football stadium renovation or whatever. What a public service. But maybe that was like, a failure to launch. Or you're just from this city, where failure is a kind of success, it's like a pH balance just for us, a failure deodorant that works on everyone here. And now I'm caught up in that again, just when I thought I had found my own thing, I was escaping Loserville, just when I thought I was striding down the straightaway, breaking away from the pack—maybe the pack is right on me. Where is Steve? Where is someone? How big is my lead?

"Angela," Krys said to me once—I'd told everyone I'd sign any document lying about the size of our hallway, I'd tell a judge hand on Bible we had an Olympic-sized pool for a hallway, and I was just off probation, who gives a shit, if they came out and measured it, I'd just act blonde, like always, eyes wide, like I had literally no idea, just so surprised by tape measures, who cares—"Angela," Krys said, "grow up. Stop pretending like you're some sort of martyr for the cause."

Huh.

Day 15

In our last convo Steve—how can there be a Stevie and a Steve? Christ. Mike it is—had said the article would be out *soon* but when's *soon*? I texted you, *like what is* soon *for reporters? also talking to this guy* (linked to Mike's cringe social presence), *did u contact him re photos?*

I'm only now realizing (it's evening now, must have been late morning then) you haven't replied. Are there other major political actions occurring in the city this week? Did some suburban mom fail to match her lipstick to the exact red hue of our racist baseball team's old logo?

Bright orange popcorn. Salty cheese dust.

Do you think if I think about food it attracts the roaches?

Scrolling around. No one else has done what Dr. M did? Just ignore the law and keep giving abortions. Or, they have, but they haven't been caught. That's what we don't know, if there's a secret army of Dr. M's. How do you decide who won't turn you in, who you can give the little wink to, the *come-back-later*? I'm sure Dr. M thought no one would turn her in.

I bet she trusted everybody. It's not that she's naive. She just really feels like she's in charge. It's not like she thinks, like with her brain, that she can control every situation. But she feels that way, and in life that's what you go by. Like, who do you sit next to on a crowded bus? You don't weigh the factors or like examine your bias. You go by instinct, by smell.

You can see why other docs don't follow her lead. 12 years in prison, bad news, shut-down clinic. Some places you can get sued just for giving a ride. Jailed for dropping off a pill. Just for suggesting "abortion" as if people wouldn't know if you didn't tell them. I mean thousands of years ago women were chewing on plants, exploring their options. They probably had the same problems. Here's a tiny kid, a 10-year-old, she can't give birth, anyone could eyeball it, try to help.

Scratch that—I think maybe people *don't* know their options. That's something we do need help with, knowing our options. That's why those crisis centers sprang up everywhere. If you could tell people a baby-story, right away, get it in there, you could build a shiny world around this nausea they were feeling, this way their body was getting hijacked. Then they'd have a story about babies and mommy and god, not a story in which abortion exists . . .

That's why I was proud of myself, if I may say so, for thinking of this hunger strike. It's not like anyone said, *here's a thing you could do, Angela.*

Angela, do you mind helping out? Dr. M asked that a lot, in her very special tone.

No, I chose my own thing. And so did she. The main thing she didn't choose was me—that I would be the one in here, after it all went down, raising a stink. Literally, it stinks in here. All those years, I was just around, not exactly wanted, but here.

They had a little party for me at 5 years on the job. No one including me thought I'd make it that long. The party was low-key but OK. Donna brought in a huge thing of flowers, there was nowhere to fit it on my desk, these tip-toppling sunflowers, eventually I put the vase on a table in the waiting room, and all afternoon Roses kept kind of wafting their faces toward the flower faces, catching the scent.

"It can be hard to keep a receptionist at a place like this," Monica said at some point. "Before you we kind of burned through them."

That answered some questions about why they put up with me, though not my questions about what the other girls couldn't put up with. I mean I'm sure the bad pay didn't help. Someone named Darcie had left a lot of notes I mostly didn't bother reading, although they did come in handy when the old printer jammed.

A couple weeks after the big law changed, after everything kicked off and the heartbeat law started rolling its way into the real world, I heard Dr. M actually scream. She was in the back. I hadn't heard this exact sound before but I knew what it was. That's Dr. M screaming, I thought. What now? What worse thing could be happening? was the dumb thought I had, jinxing everyone. But the scream was personal. Dr. M's dad had died. Her last living parent, now dead.

I had personally wondered whether my dad was alive or dead, since he didn't exactly exist. Even my aunt kept mum about that. *Your mom never told us anything*, she said. I don't know if that's true, or if my aunt was making a sort of executive decision, but I think I've pissed my aunt off enough over the years that if she had something to say, she'd say it. And I don't know what could be so bad she wouldn't tell me, since my day job exposure-therapy-ed me to all the options. *Well, just tell me if I start dating someone who's actually my brother*, I said to my aunt last time we tried to talk about it which was not recent. *Angela, you never tell me who you're dating*, she said. Fair point. But she kind of knew about John so he's in the clear, fwiw, and we don't look alike.

I'm stuck with John like Dr. M is stuck with me? That's who's here. That's who heard your little scream, Dr. M. Timeline-wise, she must have started the secret stuff not too long after that, not long after her dad passed. After the scream she came up to the front and I gave her a little pack of tissues I'd taken out of Krys's purse. I don't think I said anything. It's awkward when someone's dad dies and the next person they talk to has never even had a dad. I get it, that's not ideal. But there we were. Dr. M put her hand on my shoulder, tank-top weather, I think just for balance, her hand felt dry and hot and my skin always feels very cold. Sometimes people literally scream when I touch them, I'm that cold.

Mike called back and he had some of my same Qs, it went something like:

"Hi Angela, is this a good time to talk?"

"Sure. Never eating frees up some time."

"I have a few more questions, and then our fact-checker will give you a call later to confirm things, OK?"

"OK."

"Great. So I wanted to ask you again about the illegal procedures. Dr. M"—he uses her real name but I call her what I call her—"performed after hours, without anyone else's knowledge"—

"If we knew we'd be accessories, so yeah we didn't know."

"Right, but it seems like other people might have supported what she was doing, so I'm wondering how you felt when you found out. Did you agree with her? Were you upset that her actions ultimately got the clinic shut down? You all lost your jobs. You could have been charged. And now you can't provide any healthcare—like contraception, anything—or even the abortions that are still legal. So I'm wondering if you thought what she did was effective, or the right choice under the circumstances."

"The abortions she gave were all effective."

"Of course—but now you can't provide anything. Some people would say she acted recklessly and endangered the clinic and everyone who worked there."

"OK," I think I said.

"So do you agree? Or do you think getting arrested, getting media attention, having a big public trial, was the point? Do you think publicity like that and protests like yours may be more effective right now than the limited care the clinic was allowed to offer under the new restrictions?"

I hope I said: "People don't do things because they're effective. Like, is having sex effective? It bothers me that if I bombed an abortion clinic everyone would just get it. You could write it up without even talking to anyone. Like, that would make sense to everyone. Same if someone had walked in here and shot me in the face. That would make total sense. But if you try to do something else, anything else, everyone is like, *whoa you're crazy, who signed off on this?*"

He didn't understand, I don't think. Maybe I didn't say it right, he moved on: "Well, let's talk about how the heartbeat law works, then, and what happened after it went into effect about a year and a half ago. In your state, abortion is now illegal after a fetal heartbeat can be detected, roughly 6 weeks—"

"Embryonic cardiac activity. No such thing as a 6-week-old fetus, we're not fetuses till week 11. Anyway 6 weeks is 2 weeks. They start the clock on the first day of your last period. So before you were pregnant at all. Like, the first 2 weeks of your so-called pregnancy you weren't pregnant. So let's say you ovulate—*you* like generally, Mike—around day 14. So that's when you get pregnant, 2 weeks into your pregnancy, by their rules. Then sometime after day 28—and this is a picture-perfect storybook period for fairytale princesses—sometime after day 28 (but it could be day 30, 32, 34, whatever) you'd expect day 1 of your cycle, meaning blood. So you wait. No blood. You wait a couple more days, no big deal. Then you're like *hmm*. But at that point you have about 1 week left in which to buy a test, take it, make an appointment, get time off work, get yourself to the clinic, confirm *yep*, then get the abortion. If there's a 3-day waiting period on the procedure, that could blow your chances right there. And even a 1-day waiting period means more appointments booked up at the clinic, which means it's harder to schedule things, trust me. And lots of people don't get their period super regular anyway, and lots of people spot when they're pregnant, there's still a little blood—so they might be like, great, fantastic, I can stop worrying about that sloppy withdrawal with Mike the other Friday. Point is, no one should talk about 6 weeks. It makes it sound like, oh, you could still buy and wear and return a pantsuit in that amount of time. Nope. It's not like that. What you should be wondering is, what *is* it like?"

He was upset about the name thing. Just like Mike.

"Don't take it personal, for context my phone is full of numbers without names and those are guys I've actually slept with."

Pretty sure he also said: "You know, I've been reporting on abortion for a while, and I understand the problems with the 6-week ban, so you don't need to worry about explaining things like that. It's my job to understand these things and to ask people about their experiences."

"What's the deal, by the way," he said, "with these photos? A guy sent me some photos?"

"You can use them if you want. You should pay him or however you usually do it. He's a good reporter." (I swear I said something like this, I talked you up.)

"Maybe he's good at writing. These are a little trashy. Sorry, I get he's a friend of yours. I'm not sure what he was going for. I'm going to give you some advice."

"OK," I said. I always like to know what advice someone wants to give me, it helps fill out the picture.

"Get your friend to stop shopping these. They make you look like a joke."

"A good joke?"

"What?"

"Never mind," I said. "I'll share your feedback," though I wouldn't. I usually let things play out. If you've read this far, well now you know.

Fuck I just poured a little water at my mouth without lifting my head. Everything's wet. My mouth feels like a rat died inside me and the smell just keeps rising. I moved to exam room 4 to escape, even though I was kind of thinking about saving that one for later. Earlier today I was thinking of taking an alcohol swab to my teeth. The doorbell rang. Terrified, for a sec. But it was noon, Dr. Park. Took a long time to get there.

"There you are," she said when I opened the door. She entered very fast. Where else would I be?

"Let's get you back to the exam room." (She means 2 or 3, not 4, where I've never taken her, even though 4 is actually a couple inches closer to the front than 3, I realized recently.)

I looked across the huge waiting room. The chairs are lawless and two bulbs have gone dark.

"All the way back?"

She nudged and I leaned and we made our way. Past the exam room door, to the nook, up on the old scale. Squeeze of the cuff. Stethoscope, tongue out. She didn't react to the breath, which means either it's not as bad as I thought or she's as good as I thought.

I asked her: "Would you say I work in the healthcare industry?"

I was on the table and she was shaking a water bottle to dissolve the salty vitamins.

"Of course. You were administrative staff at a facility providing medical care."

"No, I mean right now. Like, you would you say that protesting on behalf of healthcare is working in healthcare?"

Dr. Park was wearing an incredibly charming scarf. "I suppose you could make that case," she said. "Though usually where there's healthcare, there's patients. And right now, you are the patient."

"But it's for all the future patients. Like everyone we could have treated."

"Releasing Fatima doesn't reopen the clinic or overturn the law that imprisoned her," she said, but in a kinda nice way. "And you've said that releasing her is your goal. But I agree that freeing her, or bringing attention to her imprisonment, could help other doctors and other patients, elsewhere."

"But if I say I'm like protesting on behalf of future patients who are *ideas* of people—like say all these people who could come here and change the course of their lives by getting a procedure, and change the course of their kids' lives (like the kids they already have), and their mothers' lives sometimes because that's who helps out, and their partners' lives, and their jobs, like anyone and everyone in their life, if I'm talking about the IDEA of these people but not specific actual real people in their own specific situations—then I'm in like Janine territory."

Dr. Park wasn't familiar with Janine.

"It's like I'm talking about ideas of people who aren't real actual people, like no one could meet them or talk to them or anything. The people I mean aren't even pregnant yet. They're not even in the situation yet. It's like the fucking parking-lot screamers defending future babies when there's no baby yet, just like a few cells stuck in the dark."

I don't remember her saying anything. What do you have to do to get her to say something?

Am I the same as Janine?

"Do you think she was right to do what she did?" I asked Dr. Park.

She took a while, or I blacked out a little, but anyway I understood she wasn't going to answer my question. Most obvious explanation: she didn't trust me?

"It's complicated," she said.

"Wow," I said.

"I believe," she said slowly, "in civil disobedience. I agree that those patients deserved abortion care. My questions would be" (I know she said this, not "my questions are" but something slipperier) "about the long term. What happens after. I would never advise a patient, or a friend, to do something that would cost them their livelihood and the livelihoods of all their coworkers, that would lead to incarceration, harm their own health. That doesn't mean people shouldn't take the risk, just because I wouldn't advise it. She had a right to decide what risks were worth it to her, just like you do. My questions for her are like my questions for you. What were her goals and what strategy could achieve them?"

I thought she was done but then she said: "Also, as a doctor, I worry about what happens when we do things more recklessly than usual. I've always found caution, good process, and humility to be important qualities for good medicine."

"Out of curiosity, Angela" (and as soon as she said that I was happy) "what would you say to the patient who came forward? Who regretted having an illicit procedure and turned Fatima in?"

"I'd say, regret is a feeling. Abortion is something that happened. Regret is a relationship you have with yourself. You can't bring other people into it or ask them to have known something about you that even you didn't know. I think the problem is that abortion lets you time travel, back to your regularly scheduled programming, pre-interruption, before your whole life was about to change and a new life was literally possible. And that introduces this idea, like what if you could keep time traveling, back to before the abortion. Then you're mad at the abortion that you can't do that. It's only half-magic. But that's not our fault. Anyway I think that regretting woman especially regretted, and don't take this the wrong way because I get it, that she had to pay money out of pocket and insurance couldn't kick in. I think she thought that because we were all fighting the man or whatever she should get everything for free. And it seemed like Dr. M did some procedures for free and asked some women, when she thought they could afford it, to pay. I'm guessing this woman didn't like what category she ended up in."

"And were you surprised she charged patients in need for off-the-book procedures?"

"Why should she work for free? She was trying to keep this place open. Why is the question always, was it right that a woman got paid? Shouldn't she just do anything we need her to do for free or out of love or whatever? No one expects cops to like beat the shit out of people for free, they're professionals."

I wanted to see what she'd do with that. Nothing.

She spent a while reminding me what hunger strikes do to the human body.

I told her: "You're the best doctor I've ever had. I'm just not interested right now. It's me, not you, you see what I'm saying."

"You should think about what you might regret."

My aunt (I just counted) has called nine times since I last picked up.

I said: "Dead people don't regret anything."

She nodded, too quickly, and clicked her bag shut. "I'll be back tomorrow."

"I don't get it," I said. "You'd think people would trust me *more* because I'm, like, blunt, but it doesn't work out that way."

She turned in the doorway. She seemed to be thinking, or just finally inhaling, if I was right about the smell.

"I imagine that's frustrating," she said.

"I don't know," I said. "I mean, I did want you to feel bad about it when I said it. But honestly I don't know what people should say."

I waved goodbye like I was a baby. I lay down hard. I don't know if I slept exactly. Hours passed. Bringing us to now.

I'll call my aunt tomorrow.

Blunt is my aunt's word. That's what she used to call me. I guess, for her to call me that, I must have been talking to her. Back then I must have picked up the phone.

It's been bothering me: did everyone else know? About Dr. M? Every morning they got in before me, did they see signs, something going on, did they suspect someone was using equipment, medication, someone had been in here after hours? Is that why they're not doing more right now, because they nursed that little suspicion for months and it wore them out? Or because they were part of it and are glad they weren't caught, now they're lying low? No one said a thing to me. Maybe everyone who knew thought they were the only one. Maybe everyone thought that everyone but me knew.

"Deniability."

Best if you can't admit it, even to yourself.

Very late now. You texted me whenever, a couple hours ago. *No dice on the photos. Not their style I guess.*
    Did you talk to Mike?
    Who?
    Whose side r u on?
    What?
    U up?
    ??
    Come over, I wrote.
    You did.
    "You can't mind if I pass out a little," I said. You weren't happy about that but you didn't say no. We always figure it out.
    I'll miss that?
    I won't miss anything?

Day 16

OK yeah let's be honest, I want the article to come out so the others can read it. Like Krys, Monica, everyone. I mean I've only heard from Donna. I know why but I need a little help with it. I was hoping some PR would help.

They all think I snitched but I didn't.

Does Donna think that? Donna takes the long view, I guess.

They all think I must have said something. Because I slept with that one guy and he turned out to work for the old shit-head state senator, uber-Christian Nazi hate-monster. And everything kicked off right after that. The clinic got raided, Dr. M got arrested. So they thought I must have blabbed and that's what got us. One patient came forward, sure, but right away the cops knew a lot more than that. Who talked? That was everyone's question. None of us, my answer. Their answer: me.

I mean, if we're being honest—or if we were being honest then, which I don't think we were, or at least I wasn't—I actually knew something. They'd never suspect that. Me, Angela, knowing something. I couldn't have said what was or wasn't happening, but I basically could have because Dr. M kept a fucking record of the off-book appointments. Like, they weren't off-book. She made a book. In pencil. I saw it once, in the way back of an unpopular filing cabinet. All anyone had to do was find that. She is so smart and so dumb. I should have destroyed it when I saw it. I didn't know what it was. Not exactly. But I knew it was something. I mean, I totally knew. When everything happened I remembered it and thought *shit*. She must have thought notes were safe as long as she didn't type them up, get them anywhere near her phone or the internet. So she wrote by hand, like I'm writing. The one thing she should have done was not that. Don't keep a record. Don't write down the fucking date and charge and everyone's fucking initials. Which is what I saw. Dr. M, why? Were you trying to get caught? I don't think that's it. I think you kept a journal like I kept a journal back in the day. I think you pictured the journal first, in a way, like: what if I called all these patients—all these wannabe patients—back? What if I took that list Angela made of the numbers and got a burner and . . . ? Then there would be an order, the back alley would be an office, you could sneak around but have it feel right. I guess if I say I know all this, I'm an accessory, if anyone ever reads this and I'm still around.

The cops found Dr. M's little journal. Of course they did. What was she thinking. They used it in the trial. But for some reason, at work, that wasn't enough. Didn't get me off the hook. For some reason everything was still my fault because they already thought it was my fault because I fucked that Nazi underling. It doesn't even make sense. They think I can't control myself, that I have no idea what I say or said. I must have said something (they think) because the underling and more important his boss, who's from one district south of us god help them, were there at the raid. But that had nothing to do with me. These bros would never have missed a show like that, grand finale of one of the state's last clinics, handcuffs slapped on a brown lady doc. And I don't like *talk* to these guys, there's just something that feels right, picking them up, trying it out.

I knew what kind of guy he was though. I suspected. In the corner of the bar the game was on, he was wearing a loose suit, like he was going to grow into it. I wasn't even looking for anything. I had one of those big old 20 oz beers they do there. I was wearing pink eyeshadow I'd seen Monica wear, I did not pull it off. He was watching the game and whenever something good happened he'd look around like an out-of-towner. Wanting a reaction, a buddy, clink? "Go team," I said, and tipped my glass. Then he was looking at me. This guy's vibe was so basic. It was like, *what if I / would she.* Real rookie energy. That's interesting, you must be a little sheltered or churchified or your brain's still in high school. For me, on my side, it's a suit thing. I just do not have the same rate of success with suits. I am not what they're looking for. They would rather pay? So the suit is why I made this little mistake, as it turned out to be even though nothing happened. Everything about it, at the time, was fine and boring. He was on top. I like a big weight on me, someone trying to prove something and my ribcage almost collapsing. I spend a lot of time finally breathing after. When I left I said, "Gotta go, late for my shift at the abortion clinic," and he kind of laughed. That's all I said. And I swear, to him it was just a bad joke. He did not take this as a fact or confession.

He only figured it all out the next week, when he showed up with his boss at the raid of the clinic, saw me and shouted at me, I think he called me A WHORE AND A GODDAMN THIEF which seemed specific enough that everyone asked me about it very hard. They were all like *how do you know that guy* and *what did you say to him* and *do you have any idea who he works for?* But like I've been saying, it didn't matter what I said then. No one was going to listen. He didn't, they didn't. Everyone thought I'd fucked up so that's how it went down in history.

I did steal from him, so maybe that was the mistake. Otherwise in front of everyone he'd have just called me a whore, which is more generic, maybe does not suggest a personal connection. I took this OK leather satchel thing he had. It's funny to take someone's bag because then they have to carry all their shit in their hands, like out of their hotel room to their business meeting or whatever. I emptied it first, even the little stuff, paper clips, nasal spray. I was not not drunk but I'm sure I didn't say anything that he would ever remember. It's safe to be trash. What would I have said, I saw a list of illegal abortions my boss is insanely writing down? When would this have come up in our boring evening?

Sometimes Donna used to call us *my girls* but that's over.

So I guess Janine and I like the same guys. She and I, we have the same type. The thing is not to take it too far. Is that the lesson here?

But that's not where I meant to start. I woke up late, I guess. In my opinion all times to wake up should be equally valid, especially now, but I guess people still have ideas and you still have to hear about them. I woke up to the sound of banging on the plywood out front and your voice shouting. **ANGELA.** For a sec I thought you'd stayed over, but that didn't make sense because, from the plywood-sounding noise, you must be outside. This all took a while to understand. I'd wanted to wake up and stand underneath the shower nozzle, which kind of trickles, floppy, not that warm, but why not freshen up. I've been making an effort, at least every couple days. But no time for that I guess, because I had to deal—and I can understand how bad my legs, as just two examples, are looking, I got grossed out as I got down from the table and saw how the shape that makes legs look like legs was not there, things are getting pretty bone-like and sick—anyway guess I had to deal with whatever it was you wanted me to deal with. A while later I arrived at the front door. A bright blue folding chair had been left outside, by the door, neatly. Why? I sat in it.

"Angela," you were saying. You and my aunt were both there, as if you'd just been hanging out, not something you've ever done. Wtf?

"Hi?" I said.

"Angela, you're OK."

"I guess," I said. "Sort of."

"We've been out here for half an hour, calling for you," my aunt said. "We thought something had happened. Did your phone die?"

At that point (which was this morning) I hadn't seen my phone in a while. "Haven't seen it," I said.

"You couldn't hear us shouting?"

"I was in the back. People stand out here shouting a lot, you know, maybe I don't react."

"Angela, you look terrible," my aunt said seriously.

"That's mean," I said. "Why are you two buddied up?"

You looked guilty, like you'd come over to someone's place on a booty call late at night then left and come back in the morning with that person's vaguely parental figure in order to criticize their appearance and choices. You also looked hot. You'd had time to shave and I feel like you've finally figured out that jeans should just be tighter.

"We're worried about you," you said.

You guys spent a while telling me how wrong I am about just about everything. It was cold. I mean, it was literally cold. I was shivering, in an extreme way. My aunt put her jacket around me. She said, "We love you," which was not accurate, pronoun-wise. I'm not going to record everything you two said. I try to get my own contributions down. I try to account for myself. The rest sloshes around. I think I put my head in my hands.

"Just wait," I said, at some point. My leggings were riding high on the ankle and my lavish leg hair caught the light. No shaving under the nozzle trickle. Can't balance on one leg anymore or bend over. Did you mind? No.

Someone said something about safety, etc.

"Just wait for the big article," I said. "This hasn't even had a chance to work yet. I can't give up now, when it's about to work."

That would be, I did assert, a huge fucking waste.

In the midst of this Dr. Park, of all people, walked up. I was thinking: is everyone ganging up on me? Does everyone wait till you're weak, then come at you? Like you strolling up to my decomposing ghost face with your tight jeans and hot lecturing mouth? Sick.

"Hello?" Dr. Park said, with a kind of elegant and-what-is-this tone. "Are you family?"

"A friend," you said. You introduced my aunt, graciously. I guess you have great manners. Which feels shitty to learn.

Everyone shook hands.

"Well, this is awkward," I said, even though the most awkward thing, for me—which was, in fact, the *only* awkward thing, for anyone, which just made it, for me, truly awkward— was that no one else even seemed awkward. It seemed like you all (what, are you going to show this diary to my aunt? if you ever even see it) had a way of being in this weird exact situation that worked fine. I was the odd man out. Even though I was the birthday girl? Or one of those starving suffragettes or whatever from back when (I *can* read, Dr. Park, I have a lot of tabs open on my phone).

"What are you doing here?" I asked Dr. Park, though I should have asked everyone.

"It's noon," she said. "I'm here for your appointment."

"Oh," I said. "I should fire my secretary. How is it noon? When did I wake up?"

I was trying to catch your eye on that, but no. You were looking—and this is when reality took a shit in my brain—over at Janine. Janine was walking up, ugly hand-knit scarf wrapped up to her chiseled-y chin beneath her rosy red cheeks. "What the actual fuck," I said.

"Ah, your friend is here," Dr. Park said.

I don't know what I said. I was losing my mind.

Dr. Park gestured toward the blue folding chair, me in it. "Your friend who's been sitting out here," she said.

"I've been praying for you," Janine said, and it was the smarmiest thing she'd ever said, which is saying a lot, because Janine usually talks like she wants to hold you down and tuck marshmallow fluff into the corners of your eyeballs.

"What?" I said. I might have said this like 7 more times. At least 25 total, best guess, in the convo.

"She's been sitting out here? PRAYING for me?" I asked Dr. Park.

Dr. Park nodded. "I assumed you knew." She added: "To be clear I didn't know she was praying. I thought she was waiting to see you."

"Janine," I said. "Are you OK? Are you bored? You get that you don't have to come here anymore, because you got it shut down, like you wanted. Do you not have anywhere else to go? Stop showing up here like a little pervert."

But then I had some thought like: was I talking to myself? Whatever I just accused her of was my problem too. That's a real problem with accusations these days. I stood up, kind of, and slammed the door, kind of, on every single one of your faces.

I thought—I honestly thought—there were tears in your eyes. But it was just super cold out. You were cold.

Day 17

I told you I'd pray for you

I don't know how praying works. I guess people don't need, like, consent.

Next time, if there's a next time, I should tell her praying *about* me isn't praying *for* me. If you were praying for me, you'd be trying to want what I want. In a real prayer you'd offer to switch places with someone. You'd see it that clearly, like god POV, where anyone could be anyone, like we all could picture a big switcheroo.

Rose who—there's not a way to know for sure, but we thought the same thing, me and Monica—Rose who came to us badly beat up, swollen wrist as she checked in, bruise under the collar, it was clear she'd come far, from way out past the suburbs in the country, if it's still country out there, and eventually we thought, we decided between us, that the beating had been a first try at ending the pregnancy, I mean not by him (he thought the beating was about whatever he usually thought the beatings were about) but by her. She couldn't get all the way out here, take the time off, get a babysitter, or she thought she couldn't, not without him finding out. She didn't want the kid so she tried what she could think of. She tried to get him to do it. Hurt her enough that she'd lose it. She's not the first, not the last. To use the worst thing you know to see if just this one time it could help. Better than having another kid with him. Rose didn't say all this but when she said *I thought I'd bleed after but I didn't*, you could tell she meant just that one kind of bleeding, no other kind counted. She was showing us the way to a place whose secrets she'd learned, she was kind of proud, I think, she was showing us something hard she'd figured out. "I think," Monica said to me after, "she wanted me to know."

"You tell people you're crazy," I said, "to see if they'll disagree or agree."

Rose is reasoning.

The article came out this afternoon (finally) and I read it a few times, a few hours apart. It didn't seem helpful. Was it helpful? I tried to picture how anyone else would read it. How could I know that? That would mean knowing the first thing about how they saw me, Rose, anyone. *I don't know the first thing about*—why do people say that? If they don't know what the first thing is, how can they even say they don't know it? I might know the second thing but I never know the first thing.

Protest underway at shuttered Midwestern abortion clinic
Poor Rust Belt wombs, clogging up.
One of few abortion providers nationwide to face prosecution and the first to be sentenced
Dr. M, punishment pioneer.
In an unusual turn of events
What's unusual these days anyway? I've been wondering. It's getting harder to tell.
a solitary act of protest
Was I supposed to have gotten a team together? Was that usual?
support staff position
Not a doc, not someone important.
no history of political activism or affiliation with
born in the inner-ring suburb of
(How relieved is my aunt to be left out of this? No mention anywhere)
high school education
OK. Accurate. Relevant? I mean, do people major in hunger strikes in college, making girls like me underqualified? Bobby Sands didn't get his BA but no one harps on about that.
difficult background
Is that code for something?
felony DUI record
Yup.
Her mother died of suicide when she was eighteen.
There you go, Mike.

No mention of my championship? Just, what is it, *promising high school athlete*?

Promising? Winning wasn't enough?

I texted you: *Makes me sound like some kid other kids' parents tell them to be nice to*

Sorry

No really I sound pathetic a sob story

You texted so fast: *I thought that was part of your thing*

My thing?

Yeah

No

I waited. You didn't reply. I wrote again:

No

Day 18

Hand is tired.

Shoulder, everything. Hurts.

What was that guy's name, dude from my high school? You always pretended to forget his name but now I've really forgotten it. You didn't like him. Didn't like that I fucked him. Wouldn't even ask if I did. Yes fyi. Sean? Sean. I liked Sean. Isn't it the same name, Sean/John. This fucking city only has like two ideas and then they're the same. He was in a good band you said wasn't that good, like that proved anything.

Feels like I'm moving when I'm just lying down. I have this idea like the roaches could carry me. When I need to go to the front. Like if dozens of them could get under me, make a platform, I'd glide around on those shiny backs. But we need a better communication system.

I wanna say

I liked sex with you better than most sex, but that's it. That's all I'm saying. It was reliable. Not reliable because I knew when it would happen (we didn't make a lot of plans) but if it happened it would be good.

I like when my whole head goes blank. For one minute I'm living blankly in an open space. I could get there with you. I knew I could in a blink get there, like how sometimes when you look out at the lake your mind messes up and thinks it's not water but rock, endless blue rock you could walk on under endless blue sky.

Mostly I don't regret any of the sex. Even if it's bad, if it's boring. Mostly I want my memories. Everywhere I ever was. Then I want, in the midst of things, tangled up with someone else's smells and movement, their separate life that's so close to you, it's right there, right then I want to just forget everything. Blank like a lake at the beginning.

Today started off strong. Opened my eyes. Got up, though it's complicated now, I do it in stages, like my blood is going up one of those river ladders for fish. Still felt *wooooooo* as I stood and a sort of stabby swamp cramp lives in my guts, almost down into my thighs. Like you have to shit but you can't shit, bad combo. My arm is oozing free again. Not bleeding exactly. Seeping.

Found a sponge and "exfoliated."

Found cleaner clothes. The whole wash-in-the-sink-and-hang-dry thing takes forever. My clothes are still wet and stenchy. Maybe this place is meeting one of those humidity requirement laws. I never thought about it till now but none of our windows open.

I went for the red lipstick, why not. My face already looks like a tomb from some long-ago era of vampire history.

Keep thinking about a milkshake. Coffee malt, maybe. Sucked up so hard through a straw. Cold lump of ice cream melts against the bottom teeth. Hurts.

I sat in Janine's chair. I waited for something. A car pulled up. Someone got out. Rose. Dark pink leggings and silvery puff vest. She walked up and leaned a bouquet against the wall, on the other side of the door from where I sat. The bouquet slumped a little. Rosebuds, still tight, like they were waiting to know where they were before they showed who they were. And white-pink carnations, their blowy dumb trusting faces. A little scent washed toward me, though that was probably Rose not the flowers. She turned and waved. "You her?" she said, from a distance. Like she didn't want to scare me, or get involved?

"Yes?" I said, which was my best guess.

"I used to come here," she said. "I heard you were protesting. I didn't know what to bring"—she gestured toward the flowers, their heads resting on the November concrete—"but I wanted to say thanks"—

She didn't finish because Janine was now standing almost between us, making an 8-foot isosceles. I hadn't heard her. I'd had this whole plan for the Janine moment. Me sitting in her chair and refusing to move. But she just stood there, like a menu getting read.

"Ignore her," I said to Rose. "She kind of has consequences, but she doesn't matter. Thank you for the flowers."

Rose paused, nodded, waved as she left. "You need any water?" she shouted from the door of her car.

I shook my head. Sun glare on the windows meant her face was already gone. I'd probably seen her before. Had I? Don't remember. Unless I've stored up all the faces somewhere. In a place only my dream mind can get at, pulling humans up from memory like a metal grab-arm in that arcade game.

Rose Rose Rose. What if I forgot you?

"Morning, Janine," I said.

"Good morning," she said. I'd been wondering if she'd sound chipper or serious and which I wanted. She sounded serious and it sucked.

"I took your chair," I said. Why did I say that? I should have made her say that.

"It's fine," Janine said. "I'm happy to stand."

Goddammit.

And someone else was walking up. Someone young, with heaps of hair like only young or very middle-aged people have. She walked purposefully toward the boarded-up window, took something out of her pocket, a rattle she noisily shook, then turned toward us, tucked the rattle into her armpit, made prayer hands like an emoji and bowed. What? She stepped back then lifted the can of red spray paint and wrote—I was sitting in front of **MURDERERS**, and the other board was blank except for a couple stray tags—**THANK U ♥♥♥**. I didn't know what to say. Janine kept quiet for once. When she'd finished, Rose turned back and I smiled. It wasn't like I smiled *at* her, I was just, as I watched, smiling. She blew a kiss at us and left. Janine's face is one of those ancient kitchen piles, a place you dig into to find out what thousands of years of frustrated women have been up to. Was I crying?

"Janine," I said, "do you ever wish you were either smarter or stupider?"

It took her a sec. She watched the new graffiti drip. Was she holding her phone, like filming?

"When I was young," she said, "I wished to be different than I was, than God made me. But then I learned to trust God."

"The thing you should like about me, actually," I said, "is that I never treat you like there's a man behind you. Other people think that, you know? They think you're stupid, like a puppet for the patriarchy."

"Your side believes you get to decide who women are. It's arrogant."

"Well, I personally don't decide anything. No one has ever, and I can't emphasize this enough, put me in charge of anything. Here's my question. Do you think the assholes who used to protest here are your friends or more like your enemies? Like, do you have each other's backs?"

Janine looked cute, her little crow's feet while she made a thought bubble. She didn't look like a terrorist.

"We disagree," she said. "I respect that they're on the side of life. But their strategies aren't very effective or inclusive or loving toward women. We need to build coalitions and welcome families." She added: "I've met the leader of their chapter so many times and he never remembers my name. He calls me Colleen."

"Wow," I said.

"I have a lot of sympathy in my heart," she said. "That's why I'm out here. If it wasn't legal, all these women who are struggling to hear the right voices wouldn't be tempted to do the wrong thing. I do what I do because I understand what they're going through."

A big old hybrid SUV pulled up, put its flashers on. Rose, gray hair, got out in a hurry, carrying a pallet of water bottles stacked with two shrink-wrapped blankets. The blankets looked soft and pricey. Rose put this all down next to the sidewalk flowers, then propped the flowers back up against the stack, making everything look way nicer.

"I should have brought flowers!" she said too loudly, waving at us. "I didn't know what to bring!"

"What you're doing is so important!" she said and raised her fist embarrassingly. A diamond somewhere caught the late-morning light and lent her, I thought, authority. "We can't go back!" she said. She said, "Off to pick up my grand-kids!" and left, NPR muttering from her vast departing car.

"You're going to get the wrong reputation," I said to Janine, "hanging out with me."

Janine said nothing. Janine's like a big bunny rabbit, very still when she doesn't want to be seen.

Pure predator though.

"Janine, you totally work for that douchebag who acts like he doesn't know your name. Your mistake is next-level. You think you understand him but he doesn't understand you. But think about it. I mean, we all know what that kind of guy's like when he's at home. You do what he wants while he doesn't do what you want. Which means, I hate to break it to you, but he's in charge."

"Why isn't the abortion doctor supporting your protest?" she asked me.

"I don't know," I said. Have I ever lied to Janine?

"You don't look well," she said.

"I'm good," I said.

I had another question. I don't know how well I got it across. "It's about the heaven thing," I said to her. "So Jesus dies for our sins. But back then they thought the kingdom of heaven would start like *soon*. Like, before long, definitely while they were all still personally alive, he'd show back up, burn shit down, and rule over the actual world. But then that didn't happen. Over and over, for a couple thousand years, it didn't happen. So now we're like, well, the kingdom of heaven was never about that, it was always like over there, this amazing getaway for after you die, it's not coming to you here on earth, you're going to it, later, if you're saved, once you're dead. We all live here, but the real place is over there. If you die in this shithole, if you lived right or got chosen, you'll get to go live there, in the actual real place. But what if when he didn't come back, he meant like, I'm not coming back? What if he meant, like, this is it, this is the whole thing?"

"That's not what Christians believe. Christ didn't abandon us. He saved us."

"No, I'm agreeing with you, but I'm saying, he saved us by leaving us with each other. He meant we have to take care of each other. That's like his kingdom."

"Well, that's what we're trying to do, with our movement."

I guess I genuinely thought she'd be a good person to talk to about this. It kinda blew that she wasn't.

"Whatever, it's cool. It's cool that you come to pray for me, even though it isn't. It's cool that you're coming here, that Rose is coming here."

"Is Rose your aunt?"

"What? No. Rose isn't a person. Rose is a situation people find themselves in. You could be Rose. Sometimes I think maybe you've been Rose."

Before our eyes Dr. Park was straightening her dark-gray Prius. She walked up to join Janine's and my hangout and nodded, clicking the beeper back behind her. "Hello again," she said.

"Dr. Park," I said, "what do you call a Venn diagram with no overlap? Just like two circles and a big fucking channel in the middle? Omg"—revelation—"that's two balls and a cock!"

"Let's continue this discussion inside," Dr. Park said, and offered me an arm.

"The kingdom of heaven is real," Janine said.

"No, I agree with you," I said. "I think it's real."

Dr. Park looked interested. Janine apparated however she does. Dr. Park and I slowly promenaded through the waiting room. Three roaches crossed our path, equally unrushed. I thought she'd react. I guess I thought she might scream, or leap up on a chair clutching invisible pearls. Nope, she just sidestepped the roach scuttling toward her taupe flat.

In the back, room 2, she helped me up onto the exam table. She folded the paper—this paper—to the side delicately, like she was trying not to tear it, but also like she was reading it. I was flattered.

She said something un-genius like: "You've been writing."

"Uh-huh."

"People say they feel a sort of clarity. They say their mind clears. Do you feel that at all?"

"I don't know," I said. "So I guess not."

"I don't really believe in that kind of thing, though," I told her. "I don't really believe that one moment is like clearer or better. When my mom died," I told her, "everyone kept asking about a note. Like, did she leave a note, what did it say. But the note didn't matter. What she said then wasn't like the most meaningful thing. It didn't mean more than every other thing she'd ever said. My aunt was so angry, like it was so selfish and she didn't really say goodbye. She just left everything and everyone and there was this shitty note. I tried to tell them, her whole life is what she meant, what she was saying. This was just one fucked-up moment. It's not what everything means."

Don't remember if Dr. Park replied to that. Maybe she said *I'm sorry* because that's what people say. That's OK. She means it.

She spent a while telling me about the case. Let me try to get it down, understand it. Understanding is harder.

"Fatima's lawyers contacted me," she said. "Her son as well, the whole team. They kept saying *we*. I assume that includes her, too. They wanted to know how you're doing and if you'll keep going."

I asked what she told them. She said: "I haven't told them anything. I needed to talk to you first."

Are people afraid that life might actually be simple? Do they need everything to be hard?

"I'm good," I said, "Say I'm doing good and I'll go as long as it takes."

"All right."

Still waiting?

"I think the question for you," she said, "is how you think they could help your protest succeed, what role you'd like them to play."

"OK."

"You might want to give some thought to that."

"OK."

"Are you paid for this?" I think I asked.

She looked surprised. "No," she said. "But I have a good job, you don't need to worry about that."

"Do you believe in my protest? Is that why you came?"

"I came because you were a patient in need of a doctor."

"Would you treat someone like me, like on a hunger strike, but for a cause you didn't believe in? Like someone protesting against abortion?"

"Yes."

"Do you think Dr. M was wrong to do what she did?"

"No."

"But you wouldn't have done it."

"No. I don't know. To be honest I like to think I would have been a little smarter about it."

"You think she was stupid?"

"No. She wasn't strategic, though. Maybe she was arrogant, or maybe she wanted to get caught. Maybe she thought getting caught would turn out differently."

"Do you think I'm stupid?"

"No. But you would benefit from having more of a strategy."

"Do you know what the best strategy for winning a cross-country race is?"

"No."

"Just run faster than everyone else."

"I'm sure there's more to it."

"No," I said. "I promise. That's it."

"If someone was doing something like this for me," I said, "I'd like pick up the phone. Do you know what I mean?"

"I do," Dr. Park said.

"So that sucks," I said. "I mean potentially. But then"—and this is the part I want to remember—"this isn't even about her. If she isn't into it, fine. It's not personal to her, you know what I mean?"

"I think so," Dr. Park said.

I knew she'd get it.

"What would you like me to tell her team?"

"Tell her I hope she gets out but this is bigger than that. Tell her I'm doing it like she did the secret stuff. It's not just for the one person, it's for everyone who could be that person. Can you say something like that?"

"I can."

"Or I can do it."

"They might appreciate your meaning better," Dr. Park said, a little slowly, "if it comes from me."

People always get diplomatic with me. Like they think I'm going to be offended by their little criticism but no. I'm actually only offended that they think I'd be offended.

"Totally agree," I said.

I told her I'd been reading about a guy in Guantánamo who'd been on a hunger strike on and off for almost 10 years.

Dr. Park's lipstick is pink at the edge but faded in the center, like she chews at it, like it just never looks the way she hopes when she puts it on in the bathroom mirror.

"He was imprisoned," she said. "He had to keep going because they weren't letting him out. You can walk out that door anytime. You shouldn't forget that."

"Point is," I told her, "you actually don't have to come check in on me every day, I've been reading about it. I'm not in the danger zone yet. Are you coming here just to be nice?"

"No," she said. "I'm an overachiever. And if I take my lunch break at work, this new fellow tries to join me and he's pretty annoying. So you're a good excuse."

"Thanks!" I said.

"I've been in jail, you know," I said. "Drunk driving. 30 days."

"I read that," she said, "but thank you for telling me."

"And a couple other times, actually," I said, while I was at it. "For some nights here and there. Once for drunk and disorderly, once for DUI again, for uh indecent exposure. Nothing bad, I was just pissing on the street."

"You didn't just get a ticket?"

"Disrespectful," I said. "I mean they told me I was disrespectful."

"I see," Dr. Park said. "There are worse things to be. See you tomorrow," she said. "Rest up."

You can forget you're locked up, if you're lucky. Like if you fall asleep, pass out, peace out, settle in. But you can never forget that you're not locked up. Freedom is the first thing.

Now I'm wondering: did Janine know the Roses were coming? That they'd show up today, magical, like a pop-up garden? Did she get here early? Is there somewhere the Roses talk to each other and Janine listens?

I'm getting an idea.

Napped. I'm resting up. You've been texting me all day. Like you're trying to make up for the other morning. You don't usually have moves like that. It's like I'm more of a girl now. You're scared you dropped a kitten and it ran away.

Me: *Don't you have band practice tonight*
?

Oh sorry thought this was Sean
Night.

Day 19

I feel like
 I finally have the right job.

The problem with Sean from high school—why it did not "work out"—was his brother's ex-girlfriend. Not something she did. Something done to her. I didn't want to think about it anymore so I couldn't hang around. It happened the night after prom. Not the night *of*, that's what everyone says, they tell the story wrong, it was one night after. Sean's brother and Sean's brother's girlfriend had gone camping. High-school-wise they were the star couple and this was their big romantic plan, except. She must have told him, night of prom, that she was pregnant. She wanted them to get married, classic. Later he'd be like *I didn't want to lose my football scholarship* but the thing is he barely had one. It was the local DII school. The man was not going pro. He brought a baseball bat, on the trip. No baseball diamonds, no T-ball setups in the woods where they pitched a tent. You can only recognize her by an old photo if you already know. High school kids had fundraisers for the surgeries. I think I washed cars. Of course the baby was gone, lost, done. Why did he hit her face? He must have gotten started and not wanted to stop. Sean told the cops he saw his big brother put the bat in the trunk of the car. It didn't just happen to be there. This made a difference. This was a plan, you get charged on the plan. I was proud of Sean for saying that. The truth about his own brother. His parents were not so proud. Afterward he used to go by her house— Rose's house (this girl was named Rose, for real, she was Rose)—and bring her little coffees or snacks, sit and chat on the porch. Not sure what they had to talk about but Sean is chatty. Drop him in any bar anywhere. Anyway I think that's why we never got serious. It was already too serious. I couldn't handle it, you could say. That is in fact what he said. Like a lot of people I couldn't quite take seeing her. Her changed face, her slowed speech.

Later, when I thought of her, I sometimes wished she'd come up to the window, come to this place. Then I'd have another chance. I could be like *hey* and just be helpful. But it's fucked up to want people to need help so you can help them. It's all fucked up. There was either a moment when she woke up after, or she was awake the whole time. Either way everything she knew changed. This whole volleyball world (she was captain), sneaks squeaking on the floor, meet your boyfriend in the hallway after, plan for the weekend, hairbrush and a little booze in your locker, she knew all that forever and perfect. Then one day the world was something else. What was strange was how you could recognize its new form, you just never thought this other world would come for you, and be so personal, so that you'd have to learn how to talk again, or watch the hair get so thick on your arms, feel the hot place on your skin that covers a fresh broken bone. Rose finds a lot out. She gets to know, if she lives. She finds out who comes by the porch, what happens when people find out what happened. That's what people, me included, can't handle. Not her face but what she knows when she sees you see it. What she knows about a boyfriend she gave a nice BJ to when he got his bad scholarship. Everything that Rose knows is what we don't want to handle. But I'm getting there now, walking toward that porch.

I'm getting closer.

Day 20

Phone blowing up? Piss burning? All good?

Did the phone wake me up

or am I just never asleep exactly totally?

Just kind of alive.

Lift my arm up and down, press it on the paper, where blood—the old dent—makes a pattern, interesting. Delicate and fortune telling. Now it's just blobs and smears.

Wanting something like hot broth, rainbowy fat on the surface, little carrot shards.

You know, I got faster but they still kicked me off.

Phone rang, thought it might be Dr. M and I'd get that collect-call robot girl. Instead someone just said "Hello?" slowly a few times. I guess I hadn't said anything when I'd picked up, I'd flipped the script.

Me, late: "Hi."

"Is this Angela?"

"Yes," I said. I wanted to say something clever. But then I thought this person, as just a regularly eating human being, could destroy me in any competition.

"This is Rosheen, we spoke a few days ago, I work with Steve at the—"

I remembered, Mike's follow-up girl.

"His assistant."

"Well no, I'm not his assistant."

She said something about a statement and a reaction. "We'd love to get a reaction." What? "Could you comment on the record about." What?

Went on like this for however long, a big cramp was screaming awake and I was not my best. I said something like, eventually I said, "What the shit? What are you talking about?"

So here's the statement, she read it to me, but then I looked it up so I could copy it down and get it right.

I want to know what I'm dealing with. I gotta take things slow.

Looked up her name, too, over at Mike's paper. Róisín. Wtf?

Intro stuff then: *My client has recently learned from news media that a protest is underway on her behalf. A former employee, Angela Peterson, began a hunger strike almost two weeks ago to protest the imprisonment of my client, a doctor who has dedicated her life to providing reproductive healthcare to people in dire need. Ms. Peterson states she will continue her protest until my client is free. As you know, a hunger strike is a serious action. A young woman's willingness to do something this courageous should only remind us how important reproductive rights are to so many women and people in this country. We commend Angela for her courage, and we urge you to contact your lawmakers to demand they repeal the so-called heartbeat law, which is so harmful to women and families, and to contact the governor's office to request a commuted sentence for my client. We also urge executive action on the federal level to protect access to abortion nationwide. There is no time to lose.*

Delivering this speech was a dye-job blond lady lawyer with a rich-dad coat, pearly buttons and a tight but classy shape like she'd been sewn in there. Can't remember if she worked the trial. At the end of her speech she held up—literally, in her hands, bracelet dropping into her coat cuff—a big white poster printed with a URL. There were multiple cameramen (camera-people?) so she couldn't just print shit across the screen, I guess.

Beside the lady lawyer stood a guy, tall, not old, well-dressed, familiar, oh right, every body is just made out of other bodies, Dr. M's son. I don't remember his name. I can see the point of learning little kids' names but not, like, adult children. Let's say T. That's close. He's a lawyer but not the right kind, I guess, so when his mom got locked up he had to stick it out on the sidelines. He doesn't look like sideline material. Big dark eyes. Looking right into the camera like from the prow of a sad and righteous ship.

I typed in the URL, and the link helps you reach your legislators and the governor. There's a petition and lots of prewritten emails. My name is *nowhere* on this site? Just says *widespread protest on behalf of . . .*

Am I widespread? Sometimes.

Did not sign up.

The petition had 2,161 signatures so far.

OK.

1. *More than* two weeks, not almost two weeks.

2. *Former employee* sounds like I was fired?

3. Dr. M didn't learn about me from the news. Donna and Dr. Park both knew, they both must have told Dr. M. So. It's like we 5 (5?) are supposed to just know this part's a lie. It feels nice, I guess, to be in the in-crowd. But what's the point? Is everyone in the in-crowd always confused?

Róóóóóóóóóisíííííííííín asked me like the worst version of every question.

"You heard what she said," I said. "People should do something. They should be pissed."

"What do you think about the actions her attorney promoted? Contacting lawmakers, trying to have her sentence commuted? Does that seem sufficient to you? I wonder, are you coordinating with her defense team?"

"What? No. I'm acting alone," I said. I only remembered later, like just now, that this is the phrase for like the gunman on the grassy knoll? Great. My cramps were going hard. I said—pretty sure—"I'm kind of a lone wolf out here."

Then I said: "No comment." I remembered that was the magic bullet. "No comment, no comment. Bye bye." I hung up. Definitely two *bye*s. OK.

I just needed time to think, but now I have it and I'm not thinking anything. I need time for someone to explain everything to me.

Donna?
You?

What time is it?
Fell asleep

Bunch of texts starting at 11:30 a.m. to now-ish. 3:30. I didn't have the number saved but using context clues it was Dr. Park.

Angela, I can't make it today. Emergency at work. Please let me know if you're not feeling well.

Angela, are you OK?

Remember, you can always call an ambulance.

Then a bunch more.

I wrote back: *Sorry was asleep kind of. Totally OK. See you tomorrow thx*

Now that I'm thinking about it, should I say something nice? I don't know what *emergency* means there. Here it means, like, a gun, or way too much blood.

I went with: *Hope everyone is doing OK*

Now I've got a snow day kinda feeling. Day to myself! Cramps blasting. I should go see what's happening out front. I heard a noise. In a minute I'll go.

I was dreaming about a boat, like waves slapping at it, that sound. As a kid once, just the one time, went out on the lake with a friend's dad, his big beat-up boat sitting slimy at a Midwest marina, he talked about his scavenger business? Salvager business? Of the big lakes our lake is the shallowest, warmest, dirtiest. Once in the '60s it was declared dead. Now every few summers algae goes thick and green, eating fertilizer, throttling out life. Along the bottom are shipwrecks, everyone says, from the years of dirty business, crisscrossing. That day was sunny. Seagulls squawked. Warm granola bar from a pocket, oats shiny with sugar and pulling apart. Over the sound of the boat my friend's dad spent a while describing something, a glass or iron something you could use, open at the bottom, to go down down down into the water—like if you push a cup straight down into a full tub the cup keeps a pocket of air in it, even underwater—and I thought he was making it up. Your feet in the open lake, so far down, around your head just this tiny pocket of air, this bubble you have to trust. But then years later I saw a diagram of this same thing. So he wasn't just drunk. That was my longest and only day on the water. After another year or two she and I weren't friends anymore, though I still had a pair of cheap canvas shoes with her name written in puffy paint on one side, and vice versa, unless she'd thrown hers out.

A good dream. Lots of light and splashing. But lying here I'm thinking, the dream lake sound was a real sound. OK off I go.

Day 21

OK. Yesterday. Out front: bad chemical smell. Paint. Kicked the blue chair back into the path of the door so as not to get locked out. The plywood drip drip dripped with red paint. Red paint thick & wet on the sidewalk, sliding thick toward a storm drain, down down down into the lake, Snickers wrapper twisted up in there, bird's footprint hopped out of the red mess on the sidewalk coming toward me.

I've got red paint on me somehow still, on my knuckles (how?), splattered up my leg.

When I stepped out slow, turned slow, and looked up, I saw the clinic's name was all splashed over, so that *PATIENTS FIRST* was now like *PATIENTS FIST*. I hope they do. But the red smell. **THANK U ♥♥♥** was gone somewhere under there. Rose's flowers were stomped into paint, red boot print in their dead faces. Meanwhile someone had dropped off another care package—two sturdy paper bags sat in the midst of the shit, I've got them in here with me now.

On the other side painted below/across **MURDERERS** was—in brushwork, like nice, in a spot the red paint had avoided—**PROTECT LIFE**. That's vague.

A loud noise behind me made me start. I clutched my chest like a grandma. Turned around. Siren, very close. Cop car with its lights like disco mirrors just thrilling at the red red red, like flickering it all over. Cop was getting out of the car, slow, why are they always so slow, like they're moving through bad honey?

"You're going to need to clean this up," he said.

Said this like 4 times.

What?

"Causing a problem for all these businesses," he said. Waved a hand around, like an entourage of future mayors was about to file out of the chiropractor's.

I think I said, very slow: "You understand I didn't, like, throw all this paint here myself? Like, this is a crime? The clinic is the victim of a crime?"

"If it's your property, it's your responsibility to get it cleaned up."

I suggested someone like him could investigate this crime.

"Don't worry about my job, worry about yours."

What do cops see with their cop eyes? I was like an 88-pound person in unwashed pajamas looking fucked out in front of a big fake bloodbath. I wasn't even standing really. Like, leaning on a wet-paint wall, like a junkie extra leftover from the set of *Carrie*.

My job?

"Miss, do you work here?"

Miss?

"No one works here," I said. My teeth were chattering like cartoon teeth. "No one works here. We got shut down. We were like famous for getting shut down."

My brain came through for me: "I was just swinging by to pick something up," I said. "Then I saw this."

"Looked like you came from inside."

"Well, I came through the back," I said, "then I thought I heard something out front."

"You heard paint?"

"Yes?" I said. I said: "It sounded like a boat, or a lake."

"OK," he said. "So you have keys?"

"Well, I was the receptionist. First one here every morning."

He wanted to take a look around. ". . . See if there's any other damage . . ."

"No?" I said.

"Miss, you just said you were the victim of a crime."

"The building is the victim," I said. "I personally am just here. I'm a bystander."

The more you say you're a bystander the less you seem like one?

He insisted. For everyone's safety!

I want to describe how we were even talking. I'd planted first one hand then two hands hard on the brick that makes the front doorway. I was talking up under my armpit to where he stood just off the curb, wide-legged, zippered-up, locked and loaded, red paint in a sick stream between his feet and into the storm drain, pooling up around stuck shit. Nothing looked OK.

I tried: "I only have permission for me to be here. I don't own this place or anything. And there's patient records and stuff, so I can't let people in."

(Donna got all the records though, right? I sealed up some boxes with tape, *faster Angela*.)

"Who's the owner?"

"I don't know," I said. Not even a lie. "I'm just a receptionist." Two truths.

But how does Donna always know about the situation beyond the situation?

His cop face was huge and young and slow. He was white and looked low on vitamin D or maybe all the vitamins. Takes one to know one. His hands were stupid red in the cold. Don't they give you cop gloves? You guys have tanks but not gloves?

"The head of the clinic would know who owns the building," I said. "She's locked up. You can speak with her lawyer."

"Ma'am," he said—ma'am?—he was gonna come in. He was gonna "secure the premises" and then I was gonna "get this all cleaned up."

The parking lot was bright and everything stank but I looked and looked. Donna? Monica? Dr. Park? Fucking Janine? No. Two people walked out of the Jamaican takeout place with heavy shiny paper bags. The grease reflected me back to myself. Goddamn. I was not suffering from an excess of options.

"OK" is what I said.

One of these days I'll make my last mistake.

Day 22

Nope.

Day 23

Red shoeprints stained into my carpet. Big prints, cop. Small prints, me.

When I need a wall I lean on a wall. Down the hallway from room 3 (why? how did I end up in there?) like a stoned tennis ball, bouncing slow off one side, the other side, shuffle-thunk to the ding of the double doors. The whole walking situation has gotten nasty, like suddenly your toothbrush is a dirty pointy butterknife.

Left the 12-pack of orange Gatorade on a chair by the door, little reward for getting that far. Not that I'll drink it. The reward is just to get to see it. Orange is the flavor I remember best, or blue. I don't think Monica gets the finer points of hunger strike vs. liquid diet, either that or she's messing with me. Either that or do most hunger strikers cheat? Should I be cheating? Point is, the Gatorade is from Monica, a whole nice care package left out there, must have been before the red-paint protect-life crew rolled through. Next to the Gatorade, tucked inside in the bag, a few bars of fancy dark chocolate, the super-bitter kind that everyone claims is healthy because it doesn't taste good. Dr. Park warned me already like 100 times: *There are rumors that chocolate is good for starving people, but it isn't. Don't eat it.* If I want to eat something, I'm supposed to tell Dr. Park first so we can like pick out the lucky meal together.

A note:

Angela, good luck. You're tough. Thanks for caring. ♡ *Monica*

Then her phone number.

Guess I didn't have anyone's number from work. From here. Donna had my number because she started in on my cell whenever I was more than 15 minutes late. Minute 16, like her hand dialed automatically. Did everyone else have everyone else's numbers? Did this bother me then or now or never?

Ding ding ding

Eventually I let you in.

Monica helped prepare me. I had my eye on—in my own brain—Monica's number. You were ding-ding-dinging the bell. For however long it took me. And when I opened the door I saw you through the eyes of the brain of Monica's number and I thought, Monica has no patience for you. She almost can't *see* guys like you, I think, because as soon as she sees them she just starts time traveling till they're gone. I thought you were different, you definitely weren't whatever guy anyone would think you were. And you are different, but only because we're all different. And that doesn't matter like I thought.

"Angela," you said. You had enough of a beard that little hailstones were caught in it and melting.

"Sure," I said.

I wanted to see the hail hit the red pool of paint outside, pockmarked alien planet. But the paint was dry. I wished it had all happened some other way, in some other order.

"Angela, you haven't been answering my texts," something something, "we're all really worried about you."

"You could worry about anyone," I said.

Inside, "I'm sitting down," I said, and sat on the floor beneath my window, the front-desk window, slidey glass. I was leaning my head back right below where, on another day, my face would be looking out at whoever. You went to move my Gatorade and sit in that exact chair, like there weren't 27 others.

"Don't touch that," I said.

Everything you said you'd said before, or someone had. You were like a montage with no music.

You: "I know you're mad at me—"

"No I'm mad I wasted time being mad at you."

"Are we going to fuck?" I remember saying totally clearly into whatever was happening.

"Not here for sex," you said, like a frat diplomat. "You understand you're too sick for that? You understand you could die? It's like you don't get what's happening."

"I am what's happening."

"We need to get you to a hospital."

"No one's too sick for sex. Why just the other day I gave a cop a blow job."

Someone sitting where I used to sit and looking out the slidey glass couldn't even see who you were talking to. Your face all doughy like you were waiting to be yourself. It would look like you were talking to no one. I was laughing at this. Not the other thing or anything else.

"Jesus Christ, Angela, what are you talking about? Is this a joke to you?"

"No."

". . . Did someone make you do something?"

"No one has to make you do something," I said, "if you just do it first."

I could see that you didn't understand me. And more, that it didn't matter, whether you understood me or not didn't matter at all. This was beyond a question of one sentence or one conversation. It was something more beautiful, like I'd always had something of my own. Hey who knew, my knowledge isn't waiting for you, it isn't waiting for anything. It's just mine. 1000% of it, from what it's like when a sad Nazi fucks you to the smell of my aunt's hand lotion to the moment you crest a big hill, open your stride up and catch her, whoever she is, whoever's in front of you. Whatever I know, I know. I felt rich, like I'd tossed a rock at a window and it changed into a thousand perfect cracks without breaking.

"You should tell me," you said. "If something like that happened. You know there has been like almost no follow-up to that one big article. No momentum. Everyone can tell she's not getting out and so they're just waiting for you to give up on whatever this is, if they even know about it. Your story's dead in the water. My friend says he was even going to write something else but your texts back to him are all the same dumbass jokes you send everyone. If something else happened, you should tell me, because that's a story."

"I'm so sorry this didn't work out better for you," I said.

"Ange—"

But maybe I'd thought about the cop too much, his bush league hip thrusting. Not even a rhythm. Like his deepest brainfolds were gross and off-beat. Gotta puke.

Somehow you thought to grab a bucket. I was filled with admiration, for a sec. Then I puked again.

Truth is, I've been puking for a couple days. I don't know why I kept that to myself.

I think a time comes when you no longer know what's happening.

Was I looking forward to that?

"Sorry I'm not the best at this," I said to you.

"At puking?" you said.

That wasn't it. I sat back. I wiped my mouth and tried to picture anything that wasn't my breath. Incense burning in the corner of your apartment and tomato soup you were heating, salty paste clinging to a can I scraped out with a finger when no one else was looking. I reached my hands toward you like a baby but you were gone.

"You have to wait," you said, putting a water bottle next to me. "If you drink it right now, you'll just puke it back up."

"You been researching?"

"No, I've been drunk."

I kept feeling something. Alone. There was something I'd stopped wanting. Usually that feels bad.

"It's fine not to know people, but not to not want to know them," I said.

You nodded. But not because you got it.

I tried drinking some water. Nope.

"It's not hard to understand. What I'm doing, it's simple. There's something better, something that's possible, and maybe you can clear the way to it because maybe you're part of what's blocking the path. Because there's nothing we're all not part of. Everything good and everything bad. That's how it was with my mom. People thought I'd be angry with her for dying. That's typical or whatever. I mean I was angry. But I also knew she was just making a mistake about what was blocking the path. I always got that." I am sure I didn't say this. But did I say enough?

You were still asking questions, cop article cop. "I work in media, I can help."

I can't guarantee I said: "It's like, when a place like this closes, you never know how it will fuck with people. I just want to say something about that. It's so hard to see because it's just everywhere, all these things that didn't happen. Lives are hard to see. Like all the parts of real lives, especially the parts that didn't happen, or what was possible but got lost, got blocked."

I threw up, but right into the bucket, and a little on my own paint-chip knuckles like collage.

"You wanna take some more pictures?" I said.

Bye bye.

That was yesterday. Today thought I'd go outside to wait for whatever came next. Brought my bucket. Brought a bunch of chairs, one by one. Rest in between. Wanted to make a kind of daybed, like a fainting couch, what do you call this relaxing furniture. No more sitting up. Fuck that.

Outside was not bright, but for me it felt bright. My eyes are not pulling their weight.

By the door were more flowers, yellow ones, big pinky-blues, I don't know their names. I just left the bouquets around. Did it look like I'd died?

The cop hadn't come back or sent any friend cops.

Why think about cops?

The sidewalk was kind of scrubbed?

On the building a blank faceless white had covered over the red. New round of paint. Now the clinic looked like a white carnation held against a rose. These windows were full of surprises.

This must have been why John said *What red paint?* I forget what I'd asked him. You, not him. No, I don't know who I'll give this journal to actually. Some things have changed since I started. What's been bothering me is that when I get to the most important part I won't be able to write. This whole journal-thing, which I've actually worked really hard on, is like an intro to something so important it can't be included.

I bet the other girls would agree with me, John said, trying to get me to end the strike. By *girls* he meant like *coworkers.* Funny when guys try to use your fellow girls to win an argument. Like there's a bond among girls that I, a girl, can't fight, an ancient moon logic that'll strike down a rebel.

At a weight this low you're setting a bad example, doctors said back then, like I was cheating instead of dying. We just gotta make sure all the other girls are never like you.

Anyway I told John he had no idea what "the other girls" think or what I think about what they think, fuck. But as usual I was at most half-right. I'm thinking he *did* know what they think, because they had literally written it on the wall outside, he'd probably read it on the way in. They'd signed their names in black on the corner of one white-washed plywood plane. *Krystal + Donna + Monica + Stevie +* even some other part-timers & interns I mostly don't think about. This must have been 2 days ago, early evening, the doorbell was ringing hard. I didn't get up. Whose writing? I'm guessing Krys because she used to draw those wholesome little comics for her kid, with a baseball-cap-wearing duck in them, waddling cute through this city like it would keep him alive.

PRO ABORTION 4EVER in big black bubble letters across the left window's plywood.

WE WILL NEVER GO BACK

Krystal + Donna + Monica + Stevie. They'd all come together?

I shoved my chairs around so I could really see. I stationed my bucket. I had at least three blankets. Rose's blankets btw were amazing. When I'd first unfolded them I thought they might have like clothes hanger logos but no. Too bad, that would have been metal.

Water bottle and my hugest sunglasses. I was so cold but it was not so cold, from the weather's POV it was weirdly warm? What is going on with seasons? Does anyone care?

"What do you need?" someone was saying. I gagged. Must have fallen asleep. Who wakes you up at your own protest?

"Wtf?" I said.

"We're here to show solidarity," a backlit person-shape said. Another one said, "Hello?" then "I think she was asleep?"

I figured it out. 4 of them. They looked codependent but not organized. They were from a group they told me about. "What do you need?" they kept asking.

"Just water, I guess," I said. "I have enough salt." I guess I hadn't seen people in multiples for a while. A single person you can keep an eye on but the 4 of them kept squirming around, 1 was carrying a pallet of water bottles right at me. "You can bring that inside, I guess. Thanks."

"You don't need to thank us," they said, redundantly.

OK.

"How are you feeling?" I think they said.

"Below average."

They were nice & all, but they had to deliver a little speech that made me want to say, I think I might have said, *you know, I'm not personally the internet.* Also they were like hanging around even though we didn't really have a shared activity, is this what it's like having fans?

"Ms. Peterson?" said a more interesting voice. New shape, polite.

"That's me." I squinted and saw: T.

"Is he bothering you?" from one of the circling groupers.

What?

"Thanks for stopping by," I said to the groupers, remembering my mom saying that a little bitchy to this one neighbor with her church-talking mouth. "Thanks for your support, I'm into it." Was that right?

"We'll keep up the phone calls and the petition," someone said.

"Cool."

"I have to take my next appointment," I said, nodding over at T and twitching my blanket in at the throat, like I was royalty, talking to total strangers with a chair eroding my butt bones and some fresh puke stocked up.

They swarmed off after telling me accurately that they'd left their phone numbers with the water pallet. They didn't mention they'd also left a bunch of printouts and shit, like homework to understand my own "direct action" better? OK.

T has this look about him like, if you sat down at a bar, he could be sitting there, reading a fat book, sipping a gold beer, moving his coaster with a gentle finger, and you'd sneak a look at the spine and the book would be something you'd never heard of, which made you wonder so hard what world this person lived in. None of this was happening.

"Do you own the building?" I think I said. Ladies, know your landlords.

Day 24

Fell asleep, I guess? While writing? Dr. Park has come and gone. She's talking about IV fluids. She's got ideas. "I really respect you," I said, true and a way to say no even though, as her new haircut also proves, she's got better ideas than almost anyone.

On her way out—likes to get the last word in, doesn't she—she said, "You know, you can accept help privately. If your strike becomes partial, or is in the process of ending, you would decide when and how to share that information. I wouldn't disclose it."

"Sure," I said. "But I've never cared what anyone thought."

"I think this might be the kind of thing your friend meant," she said, after a pause, "when she gave you that Gatorade."

Literally hadn't thought of that

"Why don't you give it some thought"

Like always waking up but never sleeping. T is texting something polite, *Just checking in.* OK.

Does T matter?

Should have asked those activists for like 10,000 blankets. Pls explore some blanket-related decision-making.

I want to thank you for what you're doing for my mother. Most people aren't this courageous. It means a lot.

Means a lot to who?

Courageous sounds like a kid with cancer?

T works on lawyer stuff with the internet and spying, privacy stuff. "That's great." Or "Great someone's on that." I honestly felt relieved. "I'm sorry I didn't come sooner" (always funny?) "I was traveling for work." He said where he'd been, with who, what the case was. I obviously should have recognized 100% of this. Obviously most people really reacted. To be fair I was like starving on the sidewalk weirdly lying down on 5 chairs.

"Sorry," I said. "I don't really know things, my bad."

Imho doesn't this kind of protect me from gov't spying?

Around then is when Janine arrived. This is why I'm bothering to hunch up and write, for Janine.

I remember I sat up a little more, regal-er. "Janine, this is Dr. M's son." "This is Janine, who put your mom in prison."

Janine said something about how the law, not her, puts people in prison, and also people's choices to violate the law.

I had some points to make.

I think T objected to my tone not my content.

Would he make mistakes like

they'll go easy on her because doctors are sympathetic

or

pose like this

or

it's a simple chemical imbalance

Janine looked like she'd worked a graveyard shift at the smile factory. Her lipstick was too purple for her blue undertones.

I couldn't have said, just then, what I felt. But that's not new—not special to the situation, body deciding what part of the brain to eat first.

Something had disturbed Janine. She was puffed out and rowdy like a bird at a truck stop. "It's a sin to kill yourself," she was saying.

Did she think I hadn't heard that one

"Bringing shame on"

"Proving that you do not value life, you do not value God's creation"

Me: "I'm making a choice"

"Murder murder suicide shame death"

"I'm a person, Janine. You can tell I'm a person because I'm like not the same as you, so I'm my own person, I'm alive."

She wasn't praying for me anymore, she said, even though "praying is the right thing to do when someone is suffering and has lost her way."

Then she switched horses: "You'll be done with this little game soon. You'll move on."

"Captain goes down with the ship," I said, meaning me or Dr. M? I guess both. I remember I lifted my sunglasses to look at her and mimed striking a match, throwing it back over my shoulder at the beautiful clinic.

Janine weirdly handed T some paper. "You should have this." I wanted it bad. But he just put it in a pocket. Not his inside left breast pocket like I was picturing, but folded up again then into his righthand ass pocket. What?

"You didn't want to say anything to her?" I said when she was gone. He didn't look bored.

"It's not productive," he said.

"You don't have to be productive," I said.

"More people should care about this protest," he said. "It's a powerful act."

"Well," I said. "People do starve to death all the time. I mean, I almost starved to death already once, a few years back, and I promise you more people care this time around."

I think T looks at me and thinks: *my mom is worth it.*

He suggested his mom had described me so that he "expected something else."

"Your mom has pretty specific expectations for people," I said. "Sort of gets in the way."

He nodded but he also seemed like a guy with expectations.

"I saw there's a GoFundMe," I said.

Confused look?

"On that page her lawyer made? To help with Dr. M's legal fees? I'm just wondering, if I have legal fees, would I see some of that money? The cops have already come by here. So it's something I have to think about. I don't have doctor-lawyer money to fall back on."

Apparently everyone's going to look into this. He seemed not unstressed-out. What a gentleman, he offered me help getting myself back inside. I refused. I'm thinking about it because just today, one day later, I would 10,000% accept. Wonder if I'll ever even go outside again

Day 25

Should I tell T about the cop
　　Is T who I should tell?

What's to tell?

The thing is, it's the sort of thing I know about and the cop
knows about
but who else would get it?

Soon as the cop walked in here I knew it wasn't going to be about
the paint or a fine or even abortions. It was going to be
about whatever he could get it to be about. I knew he could
lock me up. They can always lock you up. Even if later he had
to let me out—if someone like T showed up with the good
paperwork.

I don't want to go to jail.

I want to be here. I don't want to be in jail.

I could get the tube there, end the whole strike, end everything. Maybe not, because our county jail is better known for accidentally killing people than keeping them alive but still. Once you're in there you're in there, they've got you, they can shove a tube down your throat, you can't stop them.

So that's why I talked him into it. The beej

He'd say it was his idea. But guys like him are blank. You can tell. The blank ones are the bad ones. They don't have like a goal or a meaning. Put them anywhere, they're like, what's in it for me? And me, I can handle it. I can blank myself out. It's a choice. I can handle myself. You get down on your knees, whatever. The roaches are like, we've been there, we get it.

Day 26

Well

Day 27

Been trying to remember
  Get it down right
The drive home from state. I should have taken the bus home. Normal = take the bus home.

State champ on the bus. Hero = me. The girls all singing along to "our" songs. Not mine.

Plastic bags of candy necklaces we'd put on and chew at. Sometimes in the shower you'd miss a spot. Orange smear on your throat days later. In the back someone would have some vodka in a water bottle. But I went home with my aunt.

Asked my coach, waved at the bus windows, walked instead to her minivan.

Soon as I got to the top of that world, STATE CHAMPION, I felt like: nope.

My aunt is like me but different. She doesn't like talking to people, so she does it careful and business-y, she can talk to anyone as long as she can ask them what their job is, tell them what her job is. Everyone's gotta get sorted.

I felt like she deserved something for coming to the race, driving all that way, and that something was me. Whenever you feel like you're something someone deserves, that's good. Go with it. My mom wasn't dead then. She wasn't doing well. I was starting to see it in a big picture way. She'd said to me once, when I was like 12, *you'll understand when you're older.* What do you know, she was right.

"She wanted to come today," my aunt said in the car, I think it was the one thing she knew she should say, she must have thought about it on the drive over. Outside were those huge stupid same houses with endless decks where the grills turn a corner, more grill. 100 hot dogs, end to end.

My mom hadn't been too too nice when she said she wasn't coming, and I don't know if I believed my aunt then or decided later to believe her. It was the right thing for her to say so I played along.

"She's sick but she wants to be better." My aunt said things like this a lot, obvious things, you couldn't disagree. Doesn't everyone who's sick want to be better? And if you don't, isn't that just part of it? Doesn't that mean the sick has just seeped in deeper?

It's OK, I'd say. I just meant, she doesn't have to want the right thing. Let's all just let her off the hook.

5 months later she was dead. I had my scholarship and so off I went. Did she wait till I got the scholarship, till it seemed like I was gonna be OK? I think my aunt thought that too. I didn't even have to move all our shit out of the house, everyone was tripping over themselves to buy me a storage

unit they still pay for somewhere. What could be in there? It was half a house, the old duplex, and a little bit falling down. Like, wet ceiling spots and window frames that weren't really part of anything. My aunt and I didn't know the future, in the car in the fall as my sweat dried and my teeth banged away, she cranked up the fancy heated seats, I thought my shorts might melt into my thighs but I was into it. It was like we already knew. Me and my aunt. I think she was doing all this just in case. By giving me a ride she was telling me she'd give me a ride. It sounds like I'm projecting all this back into that moment. But I think, sitting there, we were scared of the same thing. And we each knew this was the best option available. She ditched out early on work and drove to a sport thing she didn't understand, and with a big-ass medal around my neck I ditched my friends, my team, they were not my friends, the whole thing, it was a kind of contract. If the worst thing happens. If you offer me a ride I will accept your ride.

I'm going to text her right now. *You're a good aunt.*

That's all. She'll hate it because she's been calling me and calling me.

Trust me, I texted, which I meant just about the good aunt thing, not the hunger strike, it's cool if no one trusts me on that.

Took forever to get out of the suburbs we were in and back to our own suburbs. Crossed a river whose name was a word I'd never heard in my life. Brown water, fake-shaped banks. All the rivers in this state have Native American names, my aunt said, then made a little history lesson, like in honor of my mom who was not there, talked about the great-great-great-grandparents of us white people coming here, driving everyone who was living here out, killing and spreading killer diseases, cheating and lying and stealing. Then settle down, get the whole suburb scene up and running. And that's not even fair, the suburbs are our thing, we can't even pin that on them back then. Killing who they were told to kill, feeling however they felt about it.

Don't know what they all pictured for the kids of the kids of the kids of their kids

Probably nothing. But here we are

Even the lake has barely made it. Even the sea they crossed over, trashed.

Not that I owe them

But I owe them my life?

Every few months billboards pop up across the city:

ABORTION IS POPULATION CONTROL

ABORTION IS FAKE FEMINISM

I mean not like there isn't a point in there somewhere?

Whose kids get what? Whose kids even exist

If you beat a guy right at the finish line in a road race, 99% of the time he asks you out after, like you owe him

Anyway years later I'd been MIA from the fam too long so I went to my aunt's fundraiser, city council thing. Pricey Italian food that didn't look slimy but I didn't eat it, I thought about it too much, wanted it too much, then couldn't eat. My dress was too shiny and way too short. Not subtle. But I didn't have another good dress, just some funeral-looking one I kept around in plastic, bottom of a duffel bag. This dress had shrunk in the wash or I remembered it wrong. I'd just do a good job with posture, I thought, if I didn't slump forward it wouldn't ride up my ass. But I slumped and it rode. When someone looked I said, *hey I'm a growing girl.*

John liked that?

I'm not proving

I think you can just try some things. But you have to really try. I knew when I took that ride with her that this would be something we wouldn't have again. I didn't want the hero shit, bus full of girls, singing like we were all on a hostage video. I'd tried so hard and I'd won. The minute I did it—walked out of the chute and puked in the grass, walked back slow to handshake the girls I'd beat—I just felt kind of over it. Like everything I'd wanted was over. It wasn't that I was too good for it, it was that both me and winning weren't enough.

You could only find that out at the end. It's worth knowing.

What I want to say to my aunt: trying is good. It's how you find out.

And maybe that's why I don't try more.

If it doesn't go like you wanted, but you tried like you should have, it's good.

Day 28

T, stop fucking texting

You know before all this I'd have been like yeah
Dr. M's son is texting me are you kidding
Lawyer types never text me in fact that's how I got into this
whole mess kind of
But now I see it all
I'm on another level now
Punching above your weight T ha

Shut up everyone fucking stop

Day 29

Hunger Strike at Former Abortion Clinic
Reaches Dangerous New Phase
Mike & John & Rosheen 4-eva
Dr. Park showed me
don't scroll anymore
so didn't know what she was talking about
sneak, you snuck a photo
"No sign that the campaign to release the doctor will
succeed"
no sign except me, photo of me, sitting on the shit carpet
knees up, forearms on knees, head on forearms
corner of photo dark tiny shiny shadow
cockroach
commenters figure it out, cockroach
you fucking snuck it
I know because I'm looking down at the ground and my tat
is right there
you would never

every other photo of me you hid the tat
you think it's so stupid
MY HEART WILL GO ON
my mom fucking loved that movie, it was so stupid
don't look at me, Angela!
and she'd be fucking bawling on the couch
while Leo sinks into the deep and Kate's teeth are chattering
Kate's cold as hell but she's still got it
got the tat the day I packed up my dorm room and drove
a suspension technically but I just up and left
did not stay
did not finish class or "file for incompletes" or whatever
passed a tattoo parlor on my drive and hey why not
thought it was funny because of my heart problem
my heart maybe not going on?
didn't think it through exactly and tattoos do not stay ironic
my arm was kinda gross like can you tattoo a cold chopstick
but they'll take your money
anyway there it is in the photo and people will
think what they think
make up your own minds
actual spit down from my mouth
mucusy spiderweb puke thread
people'll puke looking

actually have thought about asking Krys
to draw some flowers or something for me

like to cover the bad tat up, something cool over it
never asked I guess

Dr. Park looks bad (in the face) because I look bad
"No poker face" I told her
no laugh on that
Never a laugh
in the photo you can see all the bone shapes
legs
arms
collarbone
shoulder
like my skin is toilet paper got wet and packed in
ball & socket joint, every joint, everything seeable and skeletal
everything
stringy w dying
what was I clicking around in and found it
old vid of Janine
she must be older than I thought
crow's feet but good dye job
watched it like 12 times in a row
if something happens to Janine the internet cops'll come
for me
do they wear sunglasses while surfing
keep the blood up
Janine's young but she's against us then too, or she's against
something & thinks we're part of it

screaming with her whole mouth
screaming
French braid on the crown of her head
and she's sinking to her knees
sob-screaming
her teeth aren't
must have gotten her teeth fixed
on her knees, screaming into the ground
big poster beside her, bloody chopped-up
human baby pieces
Janine I miss you
this version
wish I'd known you young and rot-mouthed and wild
rolling on the ground
goddamn
that's what I'm talking about
but you got up
got a job
shitty little paradise in a peacoat
paper says there's a big debate—but is there?—about is this
a legit political thing or not
is this just like a needy girl suicide
force-feeding appropriate
Got the tube down my nose before bitches
they'll find the path if they try it, like a river is its own scar
listen for the place in you
that's a path out
they start w/ IV though remember

bc now
you could die of food

ding ding ding ding
over it
only Dr. Park now
I gave her my key or Donna I don't know
"thank you"
T texting about $ turns out they do have for me
new phone who dis

Day 30

they tried to get in
they tried
like doctors and Janine's people I think?
doctors or lawyers Janine brought? I couldn't see it
But Dr. Park
I saw in the photos Dr. Park
she's in the doorway
in an unzipped parka
wrists bracing
feet wedged in the door corners, nice boots
like it was her place
really wedged in that doorway
I saw her later in photos
I don't go up there anymore
in the photo her mouth is a bunched-up hard line
people look like they're acting but they're very real
Donna next to her and Donna's big mouth is open
EMTs, lawyer-looking woman, man pointing a finger

at Dr. Park's torso, at her chunky belt
his other hand cupped down
like petting a kid on its behaving head
you can see Dr. Park was braced hard
both hands hard, white-knuckling
you'd have to shove her down
twist back her professional arms

Donna pointing right back at him
they didn't get in

is Donna's mojo back or is that my mojo

"hospital" "hospital" "hospital"

I am saying "I am continuing my protest"
clear & loud and I keep practicing
"I am choosing to continue"
before long
before
no warning
say it again
say it
mean it

Day 31

nice to think of you all
To T: "you better help her"
"DR. PARK"
T is sad, his mom's in jail, he's a boy
things that don't make sense
I get it T
I'm on it
But anyway right now Dr. Park is your mom
do you see
what would I spend $ on
air freshener?

NO, John
"they'd have to knock this place down" I said
"they'd have to burn it down for real"
candles outside people tell me
see it in the photos on the socials

rows of candles, shadows on the white wall
you can't really see your own home
or smell it kids always say

Day 32

forgot I sent that Janine video around
Janine on her knees crying out
souls
ideas about souls
souls are ideas
T says lawmakers are "listening" OK
like a bill to overturn the heartbeat law
not passed or anything
could never pass here
just feel better news
feel better assholes
I'm glad I guess I just don't think
what
I don't think you should trust other people like that
to fight your fight
they might sometimes they do
you should trust them by not relying on them
even though you rely on them

fuck
shouting outside like the old days
FUCK YOU
not what I want
thought things would get peaceful or somewhere else
nightmare forever
pain feels like pain
that's it
pain in the ass
if I look in the dark at the hallway wall I can see
more dark
it's not light
but moving
keep moving

Day 39

heard something breathing not me
moving
hiss or rustle, rustle hiss
thought it was roaches but they don't sound like that
I must know what roach breathing sounds like since
I know what isn't it?
something knowing what was coming
something
near me then gone

I'm out now!!
I meant to say that first
it's day 3 no 4 of being out, I woke up
big fat 0
got the needle in me
mouth wet from the inside

I am in the hospital like everyone pictured for me
but no pix please I don't look good I think
I think they sort of sponged me off, baby shampoo
no more tears

OK what happened:
felt hands on my arms first, then lifting
I felt myself moved
light through the hiss
the hiss I was hearing
moving toward the back
out the back
someone was there not talking but coughing
in the fire

there was a fire, should have said that first
someone set a fire
asleep in room 2 I was dreaming of something warm
good dream
had not felt warm in so long
then I woke up & breathed
death
I think the roaches woke me, smoke roach system, get out
get out
you could kind of see the smoke even in the dark
which is bad

but then hands
didn't see anyone coming but
someone grabbed me & grabbed a Rose blanket
draped over my head, head-pushed my mouth low
to suck the good air
smoke rises
there I was
outside
swaddled
there a long time but I love time?
very cold and cough-breathing
where were my roaches couldn't bring them
hot feet running toward our walls
did I hear them dying
crack crack of the fire
fire truck ambulance
coming from a ways
god they take their time

didn't see couldn't tell or hear
in the hissing
hiss rustle roar crack—doesn't even get at the noise
who moved me?
who was there?
people keep asking
who?
someone heard or knew

OK: someone set the fire and then got me out,
like a plan
or: someone set the fire with me in there, on purpose
but someone else saw & came in & got me out

kind of the only options I guess

hands on me, bruised arms still
ambulance
I'm here now
my journal is here
hospital journal
folded up nice, tucked into a pillowcase alongside a pillow
I grabbed
& I got propped on the pillow on the ground
by the dumpster out back, swaddled
out the back
by someone
could hear the crinkle of my own words
no that part's not true I just didn't mention
I took photos of the journal all the time with my phone
I don't trust paper
that's how it survived like me
an image
not a soul

paper burns like cockroaches burn
faster

fire burned they said a long time
clinic is done
our little clinic, my answering machine voice in the cloud
in the end I had no choice
about leaving
someone chose for me to have no choice
lay me down by the dumpster
siren sound and lights found me
it was fucking cold and my little roaches
"You're OK Angela"

so one night Janine lights a match?
John? no
T no
Donna I think
my aunt? did I see white sneakers
Dr. Park??
Donna & Monica & everyone?
lit the front came in for me from the back
all planned out or just someone was watching
in another version I'm still in there that's the end
never know

never
OK
one dream me and the cockroaches shared
hell of smoke
I was light to lift
so many possibilities
nurses come in and out talking with their real mouths
beep beep beep beep
I was wrapped up, someone was running, carrying me
and running
I always said the hallway was long enough wide enough
someone carried me
just absolutely no problem w the hallway
felt heavy again and there I was
by the dumpster
they say
I was personally there in the flesh
not trash but next to the trash
wet butt and hot and cold and coughing on the ground
like a person
in the hallway
the way was clear
for a moment that way

Day 12 back to life

I forgot something.

I don't know when I forgot. But lying here I remembered.

Before the big race I was doing doubles. Running 2 times a day—morning, afternoon. So I got up real early, which isn't natural for me as we all know. But my mom helped me actually. She was up anyway, I think she wasn't sleeping much then. Things got messy by the end of the day, but in the morning she got me up exactly on time. "Ange, it's 6." "Ange, get your ass up." At some point I tried to cancel this alarm. "No," she said, "you're doing something hard," pretending like she had all the answers, "and you can't just give up." I put my sneaks on and sort of woke up on the run, slow 3 to 5 miles, trying not to get hit by a car in the dark, picking it up near the end, striding it out. I had a feeling then like I was made to be running. Not like a machine, but like a person. Sometimes my mom came with me. Not running, but in the car, driving alongside a stretch. Only once or twice, probably. The first time, she snuck up on me. She loved being a fucking creep.

Then her car was right next to me and she was smoking but blowing it out the far window, away from me, nice. I realized I must have, like seconds before, recognized the sound of her shitty Lincoln.

"Ange, you kept speeding up the closer I got," she was laughing. "Sweetie, even you can't outrun a car."

"Don't do that," I said, or something, "it's so fucking creepy when a car rides my ass."

"That's right," she pointed a chipped-paint finger at me, this cool shiny blue she was too old for, "you have good instincts, Ange. That's important. And you and me, we're tough. Everyone knows that. But you know, you can't just listen to what people say."

Exhaust, cigarette smoke, she waved out the window, sunrise pink smear to the sky, and off she went to some job.

ACKNOWLEDGMENTS

Endless gratitude to all who provide abortion care and fight for access to abortion.

To those who helped me survive my own eating disorder, even through small gestures, deepest thanks. To the medical professionals who did not help, I do not thank you.

Thanks to running friends and Coach "Do you call that sprinting" Guerra.

A scene in this novel is indebted to an essay about running that a student once shared with me. By the time I sat down to write this I no longer had the essay itself, but an echo had lingered in my mind, a delayed conversation. Thank you to that writer and thank you to all the students. Your courage is the hopeful thing.

On the history of hunger strikes as tactic, I'm indebted to sources and thinkers including David Beresford, *Ten Men Dead: The Story of the 1981 Irish Hunger Strike* (1987); Michael Feola, "The Body Politic: Bodily Spectacle and Democratic Agency," *Political Theory* vol. 46, no. 2 (2018); Kevin Grant, *Last Weapons: Hunger Strikes and Fasts in the British Empire, 1890–1948* (2019); Patrick Radden Keefe, *Say Nothing: A True Story of Murder and Memory in Northern Ireland* (2019).

Deep thanks to Diana Greene Foster's *The Turnaway Study: Ten Years, a Thousand Women, and the Consequences of Having—or Being Denied—an Abortion* (2021); Jessica Valenti's reporting on abortion access post-Roe; Katie Watson's *Scarlet A: The Ethics, Law, and Politics of Ordinary Abortion* (2018); Shefali Luthra's *Undue Burden: Life and Death Decisions in Post-Roe America* (2024), especially for details about ringing phones; and other vital reportage on reproductive rights and what happens without them.

The epigraph is from Melissa Dickey's beautiful poem "Granted" in her collection *The Lily Will* (Rescue Press, 2011).

A bow to Caryl Pagel, Lauren Shapiro, and the Hacienda Margarita Fellowship, which provided essential support and drinks. Thanks to Roy Scranton and Caren Beilin, whose close reading always helps. Thank you forever to Zach Savich. Thank you to my mom, a model for toughness.

Special thanks to Zach Peckham, who helped with research and thinking-through.

Thanks, Cleveland. Thanks, Melanie Gagich and Julie Burrell.

Thank you to Nora Gonzalez, agent; Callie Garnett, editor; and the team at Bloomsbury. To get to work with and learn from women who believe brilliantly in writing—that is luck.

Final thanks to the Teaches of Peaches, a big inspiration for this book.